To everyone who supported me throughout this journey.

Table of Contents

Satan Weeps

The First Eternity: Flesh

Tick. Tock. Tick. Tock. Tick. Tock. Tick. Tock.

The incessant hum of fluorescent lights fills the room. The clock marches on. I use it to count my breath. *Tick.* Inhale. *Tock. Tick. Tock.* Exhale. Slow. Unsteady. My heart seems to stutter as I take another shaky breath.

I never thought I was going to die young. I guess nobody does, to be fair. It was always one of those, "it could never happen to *me*" kinds of things. But here I am, rotting in a hospital room, unable to so much as piss without help.

To be honest, I've lived a pretty unremarkable life. I always pushed everything off. Always thought I would have more time. Always thought I'd have time to fix everything.

I've done things I regret. Everyone has, to be fair. I've said things I wish I could take back, done things I wish I hadn't. I don't think I qualify as a bad person, but I definitely have my fair share of mistakes. Some of them led me to being where I am right now.

A sigh slowly escapes my lips. I had wanted much more from life, but now I'm here. Dying alone in a hospital room without a window, with a scratchy blanket and an uncomfortably hard bed.

At this point, I'm just waiting to die. There's really nothing I can do to stop what's happening, it's not the kind of thing that you recover from.

There's not much else to do these days but sit and wait. I'm not afraid of dying. I don't think I have been for a long time.

The terror wears off pretty quick after getting such a damning diagnosis.

I'm not a religious man, but a quiet prayer plays through my mind. I just want to stop hurting.

The First Eternity

I wake with a start, cold sweat drenching my body and my pulse thrumming in my throat. My chest feels tight, barely expanding as I suck in air as hard as I can. I fall off my bed, landing hard on the floor.

I feel like I'm having a panic attack and a stroke at the same time. My whole body seems to be angry, twisting and grinding.

I curl into a ball, slamming a hand against my chest in a feeble attempt to ease the pain. I curl harder, trying to escape the agony.

I feel my bones grind against each other until they crack. I feel my tendons tear and my muscles rip into ribbons. My jaw clenches hard enough to shatter my molars.

I feel every single nerve ending unravel itself. Each and every blood vessel bursting apart, my spine seeming to push its way up toward my skull, curving drastically as it pushes up, up, up and into the bottom of my jaw.

The pain is unbearable. I think I am screaming but think I no longer have lungs to fill with air. My very existence feels like an affront to nature, my body splitting apart into a hellish abomination made of flesh and bone.

My jaw cracks, splitting down the middle. I feel the gap widen as my skull begins to expand, segmenting before unfurling. My very soul wails in agony, but I know it falls on deaf ears. Or no ears at all.

Where are the doctors? Where's my nurse? Where is anybody who could walk into the room and witness what's happening, and at least try to help me?

I wonder which angry, wrathful God I accidentally prayed to that would hear my plea for relief and hand me this instead.

I am crying, though I don't know if it's tears, blood, or some other bodily fluid leaking through my eyes. Eyes that are now facing opposite sides of the room.

I can feel my brain exposed to air. I know it shouldn't physically be possible, but I can *feel* every groove as the AC blows stale air through them.

I pray to gods I never believed in for help. Screaming into the aether for someone to save me… or kill me. I cry out for something to save me from this prison of flesh I have become, to let me out, to free me from this.

Nobody responds. Finally, I realize

I'm in Hell.

The First Eternity

My prayers run empty. I'm out of words to say, deities to pray to. How long have I been here now? How long have I been stuck as a monument to suffering? A disgusting amalgamation of every kind of discomfort, every flavor of pain… A criminal violation of my very physical existence.

A physical existence I no longer want to be a part of. My eyes have drooped too far to see the clock. I don't know if it has been days, weeks, even years, or just mere seconds. I yearn for escape.

My brain throbs with every beat of what used to be my heart. The stale air flowing through the grooves of my mind feels violating in a way unknowable to the living.

Living. Am I living? Have I died? It took me until now to realize that I don't consider myself to be alive anymore. Even though thoughts run through my head and I can feel every single nerve in my entire body, I don't think I'm alive.

I try to take a deep breath. I feel my lungs start to expand, but stop. I guess they popped. It doesn't matter, the deep breath helps calm me, at least a little.

I realize struggling is only causing me more pain. Like a dog in a bear trap, the more I tense, the harder I thrash, the more agony shoots through my desecrated body.

My body stopped moving on its own, stopping twisting and grinding. The only thing moving me is me. So,

I let myself sit.

Relax my jaw. Or, whatever's left of it.

Let my tongue sit loose. I feel it fall between the halves of my jaw, hanging down in front of my throat.

Slowly, gently, I let each remaining muscle fiber relax.

I feel the tension fade out of my legs, which seem to have split into hundreds of tendrils that snake across the floor like roots. I don't know what they're searching for, but I really could not care any less.

It takes hours, but finally, I'm able to just sit. To let my body relax. I let myself exist here. Without tensing and thrashing about, the sharp, piercing pain fades into a dull ache. It's uncomfortable and painful, but not unbearable.

I was dying for years before this, I'm used to being in pain and discomfort. Not like this, but still. I just have to get used to this like I got used to that. The hope of adjusting to it is the only thing keeping me sane.

I sit still for days.

My pulse slows. The throbbing in my ears subsides. I can hear again.

A gentle tune fills my mind. I realize my esophagus is whistling, contracting and expanding on its own. It creates a steady hum, a hauntingly beautiful instrument. Since I no longer control my esophagus, I choose to simply listen. I enjoy the music it creates. It gives me something to do besides sit still and think about the pain I'm in. The tune is familiar, but I can't tell exactly where it's from.

I sit still for weeks.

Hours melt into each other. Part of me wonders if I'll stop existing if I stop thinking for too long. I can hear the faint tick of the clock over the hum of my throat. It helps to count the time, but I always stop when I hit ten thousand.

I sit still for months.

I have begun to decay. I'm still sitting without tension, not a single part of me has moved out of place. Regardless, my flesh has turned sour and rotten. Many parts of my body have simply wasted away. I find myself being grateful my nose got torn apart when my skull split into a flower.

I sit still for years.

I start counting the clicks of the clock again, but this time, I don't stop.

One.
Ten.
One hundred.
One thousand.

Ten thousand.

One hundred thousand.

One million.

Ten million.

One hundred million.

One billion.

I don't know how long I've sat here for. I can't do the math in my head to figure out how many minutes, how many hours, how many days I've sat here counting. All I know is that it has been ages.

Either my nerve endings have all died or I've gotten accustomed to the pain. For the first time in an eternity, I feel… nothing. No more pain. In a strange, fucked up way, I got what I prayed for.

Without the pain, it's not so bad. The air flowing through my brain has stopped feeling so violating. It's still a revolting sensation, but it's familiar by now. I resign myself to quiet contentment. I could spend eternity like this, especially if I stop desperately holding on and let my mind fade. More than it probably has already, anyway.

There's a strange freedom in being stationary. In being an unmoving fixture, a part of the background. By this point, I'm nothing more than a decoration that produces a haunting melody. And to be honest? That's alright.

Grief is an odd process. No matter how long it takes, acceptance is finally reached. I accept this existence. I'm certain I've found myself in Hell, but I don't mind. There are worse places to be, surprisingly.

Like this, at least I'm not in pain. I don't have to deal with doctors. I don't have to hear another set of test results that just confirm how fucked I am. I don't need to push a button to get help every time I need to piss.

I close my eyes, letting myself rest. Letting my mind rest. Letting it go quiet. My thoughts fading into the abyss, leaving behind an empty void. Falling to sleep for the first time in forever.

A city ablaze. Unbearable heat turns my skin to ash but I am unable to die. The sky has been torn to pieces, the very foundation of existence shattering like glass.

Feathers fall like meteors, decimating the city of flame. A figure descends through the crack in reality. An impossibly bright glow descends with it, covering the burning world with soft yellow light. As I catch a glimpse of the figure, the glow tears away my sight.

An eye.

A voice in my mind. In my body. In my very soul. It rings through me, the sound bouncing throughout every part of me.

"Find him."

I'm awake but I keep my eyes closed. I don't want to face the world just yet. I know I had a strange dream, but I can't remember what it was. The fog in my mind slips away, the sleepiness going with it.

Something is off but I can't tell what it is. It's bothering me but I can't quite place my finger on it. It's just starting to frustrate me when it hits me.

I feel something.

I haven't felt something in years. I frown, or at least try to. I've forgotten how to after so long.

I feel it under my legs, but not the tendrils I've grown accustomed to. Under my actual legs. And under my ass. I thought that fell off ages ago.

Slowly, carefully, I open my eyes. I blink, disoriented. I forgot what it was like for them to be facing the same direction. It takes me a minute to adjust to seeing like this again, but it's like riding a bike; you never truly forget. Or so I'm told. I don't remember what a bike looks like.

Regardless, I look around the room. I'm on the bed, and I'm back intact. I look down at my hospital gown and legs. I blink, hard. I don't know how or why I was freed from the Flesh Flower, but I was.

I look to my left. The Flower still stands, continuing to hum its tune. I am both disgusted and fascinated. It's odd to see yourself in such a state, a body you've known as your own for so long in such a mockery of the human form. At the same time, it's disturbingly beautiful.

I slide off the bed. The tendrils along the floor gently slide across the skin of my feet as I walk toward the Flesh Flower, almost like a hug. I stop in front of the bulb, my brain sitting front and center. It pulses and… glows?

It's a horrifying sight, but oddly comforting. This has been me for longer than I was alive. It freed me from pain. I have… mixed feelings about leaving it behind. I'm glad to be free, but it's still a little sad.

I gently grab a petal, which is a flap of my skull, and slowly stroke it with my thumb. I pat myself on the neck before turning to walk out of the room. I pause. Was that necklace always there?

I turn back around to study it. It's been so long that I forgot what I had been wearing. A little silver necklace, a heart shaped locket at the bottom. I try to open the locket but it refuses to budge.

I carefully reach around the Flower's neck and unclasp the necklace. I wrap it around my own and lock it in place. The little heart it warm. It may just be my imagination or a phantom caused by having nerves again for the first time in forever, but it feels like it beats softly.

My gaze settles on the Flower again. I don't know if some version of me is still trapped in there or not. Either way, I'm strangely grateful. The Flower was an awful experience, but it answered my prayer. My pain had stopped, and it still wasn't back.

I open the door to my room and step into the hallway outside. It looks… off, somehow? I can't quite recall what it looked like before, but it feels like something is different.

I look to my right, and find a wall a few steps away. I don't think that was there before.

I try the handle on the door across the hall, but it doesn't open. Pressing my ear against the door, I hear a faint hum, playing a quiet melody. I wish the best to whichever poor soul may be stuck there.

Turning to my left, the hall seems to stretch forever. Off into the horizon, I see doors upon doors lining the hall. With nothing else to do, I start walking.

After spending a lifetime as a Flesh Flower, long stretches of time have stopped bothering me so much. It's refreshing to walk again, to feel my leg muscles contract and release with every step. Every door I pass, I hear a familiar hum coming from inside.

I stop and listen every once in a while. Each tune is unique, almost like the fingerprint of each Flower. Some are strained, loud, harsh, and out of tune. I imagine they're the ones still struggling, still tensing and trying to escape.

Some tunes are gentle, soft, and beautiful. It almost sounds like the song of a soul, the story of the person being played in an instrument made out of their physical existence. It's almost poetic, in a harrowing way.

I walk for hours. I try the handles on one of the doors every once in a while, but they're all locked. I keep going. One foot after the other. It must've been miles by now, but I don't mind the burn in my legs. It's refreshing to feel it again, almost like a nostalgic memory of a childhood home.

As I walk, the doors get further and further apart, the melodies of the Flowers growing louder and louder. I make a game out of trying to hum along, trying to predict the melody.

It feels like getting to know somebody. It's a first conversation, it's a last goodbye. A story around a campfire and an autobiography. It's everything a person is, summarized into a tune.

Sometimes, when I hum along, the tune grows louder. It's almost like the Flower is happy to have someone to join the song. Some of them even match my tune if I start humming something different.

The hall keeps going, further and further. I notice that a light is flickering on the horizon. I speed up a little, excited at the prospect of something different than the same hospital hallway I've been in for the past hundred miles.

The closer I get, the more flickering lights appear. By the time I reached the first light, I found a horizon full of pulsing ceiling LEDs. From a distance, it looked almost random, but up close I realize that they're moving in a pattern. The first one lights, and by the time it turns off, the next is on. The light is almost running into the distance, guiding me.

I keep walking. The doors have stopped appearing along the hall, the walls remaining bare. The further I get, the further apart the lights grow. Some lights get skipped, creating the illusion that the light is slowing down.

The darkness gets thicker and thicker as I walk. Before long, I reached the last light. I stopped underneath it to count. It turns on every two minutes, lasts for five seconds, and turns off again. Every light down the rest of the hall stays off.

Taking a deep breath, I walk into the dark. A handful of steps in, I slide to my left, placing my hand on the wall. I use it to keep my balance and to guide me forward, as I can't see at all anymore.

The only light comes from the locket wrapped around my neck. It gives off a faint glow, a soft warm light. It's not enough light to see anything other than my chest and the top of my hospital gown, but it's comforting.

Once again, it's one foot after the other. One step. Then another. Then another. Then another. Back and forth, over and over. I start counting my steps. I've gotten good at counting.

One.

Ten.

One hundred.

One thousand.

Ten thousand.

One hundred thousand.

And at last, I see it. Faintly, off in the distance, a light. A gentle pale blue light. The closer I get, the more I can see. It's a glass door. A glass door leading outside into a forest.

I break into a sprint. I stop counting my steps, too excited by the prospect of getting out. The cramped walls of the hospital have become suffocating, bearing down on me.

The suffocating feeling isn't just in my head. The closer to the door I get, the closer the walls come. The hall wasn't narrowing, the walls themselves were *moving*.

The building doesn't want to let me out. It doesn't want me to be free. I run faster, arms swinging and legs pumping as I fly down the hall. The concrete cracks and screams as the walls close in on me. The walls graze my shoulders as I run past.

I slam into the door at top speed, trying to throw it open. I push, and it doesn't budge. I pull, and nothing happens. The walls have gotten close enough for me to have to tilt to the side.

I throw my fist into the glass of the door, leaving blood and a small crack across it. I hit it again. And again. And again. After one last hit, the glass shatters. I'm barely able to breathe, the walls pressing into my ribs.

I shuffle closer to the open door and barely manage to throw myself outside. A roar screams out into the forest, the walls livid at my escape.

I suck a breath in, feeling blessed at breathing fresh air instead of the stale hospital air I've had for the past forever. I sit on the ground and take a moment to catch my breath..

I glance around, taking in my surroundings. The hospital itself sits behind me, forest blocking my view on every other side. I'm sitting on a road that dives straight into the woods before melting into the darkness. Off to my left is an old sedan, half of its bumper missing and rust lining every crevice. The Moon shines down on me with malice.

I stand up and waddle over to the car. My legs feel weak after all of the walking. Now that the adrenaline has faded, I feel like I could sleep for days.

I try the handle on the car door, and to my surprise, it pops right open. I slide inside and look around. The keys aren't in the ignition, nor are they under the mirror flap on the top of the car. I frown. I check the glove box and find them hidden behind an insurance paper and a travel pack of tissues.

I toss the keys into the cup holder, lock the doors, and crawl into the back seat. I curl up into the backrest and let myself drift off to sleep.

I'm woken up by the sound of one of the door handles being pulled. It takes a second for my half-asleep brain to register what the sound was, but once it does, I sit up in an instant and look around in a panic. I see nothing, but every handle on the car is rattling. The window to my left cracks.

I throw myself into the front seat, slam the keys into the ignition, and pray that the car turns on. The engine sputters for a second before kicking to life.

I kick the gas as hard as I can and the car lurches forward. The wheels grind against the ground but the car doesn't move, seemingly pressed into something I can't see. The handles stop rattling. A handprint presses into the windshield, fogging up the glass around it. Then another. Then another. A hand dents the hood. A spiderweb snaps across the windshield, the glass nearly falling out of its socket.

I twist the wheel to the right and the car shoots forward. I course correct and speed down the road as fast I can, my heart thundering in my chest.

The Second Eternity: Time

The road is steady and smooth. The car, despite being ancient, runs perfectly fine. The only light comes from the headlights. The forest canopy is too thick to let any wicked Moonlight in. The road itself winds through the forest, gentle curves shifting the path every once in a while.

Compared to what came before, this was downright pleasant. I drive for hours before I try to pull over to sleep. I imagine I'm far enough away from whatever the hell that thing was for me to sleep safely.

I tap the other pedal and

The brakes don't work.

The brakes.

Don't work.

I try again and again but they just don't work.

I pull the emergency brake. Nothing.

This is another fucking test. Another punishment. I thought it was a gift, but no. Of course it wasn't.

I keep driving. I don't want to crash the car to stop it. I don't want the invisible thing with too many hands to get a hold of me, and I don't know if I can die twice but I don't want to find out.

The absolute last thing I want to do is go back to the hospital. Being a Flesh Flower was an experience that gifted me many things, but it's one I'd rather never repeat.

The road stays as soft as ever, not changing in response to my realization that it's a punishment. It's still gentle and kind, almost like it's mocking me.

I drive for hours, maybe more than a day, gliding along the road. If it weren't for the knowledge that this is some kind of divine retribution, it would almost feel like a roadtrip.

I try taking my foot off the pedal to let it gently roll to a stop, only for the car to maintain its speed. On the bright side, I don't have to worry about holding the gas anymore, I guess.

I can feel exhaustion tugging at my mind. My eyes feel heavy, every atom of my body wants to collapse. Fear and spite keep my eyes open. I'm finally free from pain, I refuse to go back to being a Flesh Flower.

I count the seconds again. Nothing else for me to do, it doesn't seem like the road is going to end anytime soon. It's almost comforting to be counting seconds again. I had been doing it for so long, it just feels right to keep doing it.

Hundreds of seconds pass. Thousands. One million, two. Compared to before, it passed in a flash. Right before I hit three million, I see a light ahead. An opening in the forest.

I feel excitement jump into my throat. Maybe there's a way to stop the car here. Maybe there's somewhere for me to sleep. Maybe a hot shower, a warm bed, and a nice bowl of soup are sitting in a little cottage right outside the forest, just waiting for me.

I speed up as I get closer, my excitement eating away at me. I burst out into the opening just for the car to immediately grind to a halt.

Sand. Dark grey sand, almost black, For as far as the eye can see, in every direction but backwards. I step out of the car, looking up at the cursed Moon. It glares at me, sadistic joy in Its eyes.

Looking off opposite the entrance to the forest, I see nothing. The sky has no stars. There are no lights except the Moon and the headlights of the car.

At this point, I'm used to doing the same thing for long stretches of time. How bad could this possibly be? I take a deep breath and set off into the desert.

Walking in the sand is mildly frustrating. It requires just a little bit of conscious thought so I don't trip, something that gets in the way of me zoning out and just moving like I had done in the hallway and the car. Each step feels heavy and slow.

I walk until I can't see the shine of the headlights anymore. I stop for a moment and look around, hoping to spot a trace of civilization.

The second I stop, I hear a noise in the distance, coming from behind. Loud thudding, like someone slamming on a massive drum. It's a steady beat, but an incredibly quick one.

Frowning, I turn around and squint into the distance. The Moon is setting, taking almost all of the light with It. The thudding gets louder.

I can't spot the source of the sound. It doesn't seem like anything is moving. Not until it gets far too close. I see a shadow, moving blindingly fast, scampering toward me. It looks like a hundred arms glued to a ribcage. The arms writhe like tentacles as the thing sprints toward me.

I start to run. The moment I move, the thudding stops. I pause for a second, and it begins again. Grimacing, I keep moving forward. Seems like I don't get to stop and rest until I find somewhere safe to hide.

The Moon sets and darkness swallows the world. I stumble through the dark into the horizon. The faint glow of the locket is the only thing I can see. It might just be my mind playing tricks on me, but it looks a little brighter than before.

I keep moving, not sure where I'm heading. I can't exactly stop, and I know I'll get somewhere eventually.

I've realized something after all of the previous tests. They may seem to go on forever, but they never do. There's always an end. Barring the first, where I couldn't move, so far all I've had to do is just keep moving forward.

There has to be an end eventually. Some way to get out of Hell. Maybe gates guarded by a three headed dog, maybe a ladder in the middle of this desert that stretches into the sky, maybe something far more nonsensical. Doesn't matter. There's a way out somewhere, and I'll find it if I just keep looking.

I walk until the Moon rises again. It laughs at me when It sees me. I don't know why.

Being able to see now that the Moon is back, I get a better grasp on how far I have to go. In the beginning, the sand was mostly flat, like a small beach stretched to fill a horizon. As I keep moving, the sand gradually begins to form into dunes. More proof I'm right about there being an end.

The Moon sets and rises. Sets and rises again. When It sets once more, I start counting, as I've grown so accustomed to. I count seconds until 60, then count minutes. Count minutes to 60, then into hours. Normally, I just stick to seconds, but I'm curious if the Moon is moving like the one I'm used to.

From Moonset to Moonset, the Moon takes twenty three hours, fifty six minutes, and four seconds. I don't know if that's how the normal moon works, but it's close enough to 24 hours for me to consider it as a day.

As I walk, the dunes grow higher and higher. Steeper and steeper. Instead of counting seconds, I count days. Despite how much the Moon sneers at me, It's useful for tracking time.

The dunes keep growing. It's to the point I have to climb them on all fours, as if they were mountains. They're getting close to mountains in size by now.

Thirty days in and each dune is larger than any mountain I've ever seen. It takes a few days to climb up and a few more to go back down, before going right back to it.

It's kind of fun, actually. I race myself to see if I can climb the next one faster, even if it's higher. I still don't know if it's possible for me to die again, and out of fear of having to start all over, I refrain from simply sliding or throwing myself down the dunes.

A year in. The dunes are completely vertical. Climbing them is much harder now, as I have to dig my hands and feet into the dune itself to make any progress. Strangely, the sand doesn't fall down past me. It falls back into the dune, like it has its own gravity.

By the second year, the dunes are impossibly large. They're tilted at an obtuse angle, making it incredibly difficult to climb them. Multiple times, I've slipped down to the bottom and had to restart. These slip ups tell me that I can still feel pain, though the possibility of death is still an uncertainty.

Every slip fills the Moon with sadistic joy. Its laugh pisses me off, but I can't exactly do anything about it. I've tried telling It off before, but that just makes It sneer and laugh harder.

As I crawl up a dune large enough to swallow the sky, a thought strikes me. The sand. The dunes are angled impossibly, but the sand doesn't fall.

This place I've found myself in clearly doesn't follow the same rules as the world I'm used to. I frown to myself. I've been trying to climb these dunes, but maybe that's the wrong way to go about it.

I stand up on the dune, as if it were the ground itself. My feet stay stuck on the sand, sinking in slightly. I take a few steps and nothing changes.

I sigh. Of course gravity is fucked up here. I've been climbing so many dunes that I could've walked over. I hear the thudding in the distance and start to walk again.

There is always an end, a next step. A building, a new path, a different environment, there's always something. I just have to keep going, and I'll get there. There has to be an end.

There has to be.

A decade has passed, by my count. The dunes grow in different directions every time. Sometimes their peaks are below me, sometimes above, sometimes tilted to a side. There doesn't seem to be any rhyme or reason to the dunes. Some dunes come out of other dunes. I decide it's not worth questioning.

For the first ten years, my thoughts were filled with my next step. What do I do? Where do I go? Why are the dunes like this? Why does the Moon seem to hate me so much? How long until I reach the next step?

I am beyond exhaustion. Sleep deprivation tears at my mind, but doesn't seem to be able to kill me. As the years have gone by, the exhaustion has only grown worse. My body feels heavier with each passing second. I haven't had time to rest or to properly think about any of this. I've been moving nonstop since I woke up in the car.

But I clearly have time. I've grown accustomed to walking on sand, and the feeling of it tearing at the flesh on my hands and feet. Walking here doesn't take the same attention that it used to.

My mind wanders to the life I lived. To how I got here. I realize I just accepted that I got sent to Hell. But why? What exactly did I do to deserve that? Sure, I wasn't a saint, but I wasn't *evil* by any means.

I don't know which afterlife this is, which faith's divine punishment I am trapped in, but I don't think it really matters. I wasn't perfect, but I didn't do anything to deserve this.

I would like to think I'm a good person. I've made mistakes and poor choices. I've been shitty to people who didn't deserve it. I've been the problem in relationships. I hit a dog with my car on accident once, I think. It's been so long it's kind of hard to remember every detail.

And I think I suffered enough when I was alive. The whole point of a punishing afterlife is to make up for your crimes, right? A karmic reset? A way to make sure bad people get their comeuppance?

I rotted in hospitals for years. The smell of hand sanitizer is burned into my memory, even after all of this time. I barely remember what it was like to not be surrounded by scrubs and face masks when I was alive.

I suffered for my mistakes enough when I was still living. Was there really a need to make my body tear itself apart until it turned me into a fucking flower?

Or this shit. Eternal desert. I'm sure there's some literary significance to the desert as a concept, but whoever's in charge of this afterlife seems to be missing the point a little.

What's the point in suffering for the sake of it? What could I possibly have done to earn a punishment this severe? I wasn't perfect but I wasn't a monster. This is the kind of shit you'd see in a story about the worst person to ever live.

I feel anger rising in my chest, my head getting hot and my throat tightening. I keep walking, furious at whatever divine creator decided *this* was a fair punishment for me.

I'm grumbling to myself and stomping into the sand like a toddler because I don't know how else to voice my frustration to the aether. I hear the Moon laugh and turn to tell It to fuck off when I spot it. In the distance.

Something's glowing.

My anger fades immediately. Did I find it? The way out? The way to the next step? I'm so ready to be done with sand forever.

I start walking faster. I start to run for the first time in a long time. Sleep deprivation has been dragging me down but in this moment, I can't feel any of it. I'm finally making proper progress.

The Moon sets for the five thousand two hundred and fifty sixth time. The glow on the horizon remains. It wasn't a trick of the light. It's there. It's really there.

I let out a laugh. I've never been happier to see a nondescript glow in the distance. All of my problems seem to have faded away. I whistle to myself as I walk, copying the tune I made as a Flower, happily making my way toward progress.

Days pass. Then weeks. It's close enough for me to make out the general details now. I'm buzzing with excitement. It's getting closer, slowly but surely.

Every time the dunes make gravity change direction, the glow moves with them. I take that to mean it has to be reachable eventually.

Years go by. It's close enough for me to read the writing on the signs. I giggle. Not much longer now. Not much longer at all.

The closer I get, the more often the Moon laughs at me. It doesn't bother me anymore. I'm almost free of Its stupid, sadistic, evil little laugh. The way out keeps growing. The signs are larger than I thought, each letter seems to be about the size of my body now. I realize just how massive it is. I keep moving.

The Second Eternity

It's been a hundred years since I got out of the car. I still haven't reached the way out. It just grows infinitely larger the closer I get. Still, it's an escape. I don't care how long it takes to search the place, I'll get there and find the exit.

A hundred years since I spotted the glow. If I squint, I can see the molecules that make up the entryway. Orbs spinning around orbs, locked closely together to create the foundation of the way out.

A million years since I left the car, each atom hangs in the sky like the Moon. The Moon is still here, watching and laughing. It looks different. Cracked. Old. Withered. Still, It laughs at me with hatred in Its heart and shines down on me with malice.

A single atom fills most of the sky now. The Moon still cycles, sliding in front of the atom. I keep walking. Not much else to do at this point, no sense in turning around.

I have transcended beyond exhaustion. My body craves rest, craves sleep, but doesn't require it anymore. My legs move on their own. I don't think I can stop if I try. I realize how similar I have become to the car, ancient and incapable of stopping. The thought is almost amusing.

31

Whatever the hell makes up protons and neutrons swirl overhead. I never learned about it in school, and if I did, I forgot it a few hundred thousand years ago.

The Moon hangs dead in the sky. Its malicious shine has faded to a faint glow. Its corpse still rotates this plane of existence, the days never ending even though the timekeeper has long since passed.

In a strange way, I miss It. Even though Its laugh was aggravating, It was the only company I had. Now I'm completely alone in a seemingly endless world that is rapidly fading into the dark.

I stopped keeping track of time. I walked for so long that the particles overhead vanished into nothing, then kept walking for a few million years.

Time lost all meaning. What was the purpose of keeping track of how long I was walking for? By the time I had the chance to stop, it would've been so inconceivably long that it's pointless to even bother.

I repeat my name in my head. Over and over and over and over. I don't need time. I just need some piece of myself. Something to remind me that I'm alive, or something close to it, and I'm still me. No matter how long passes, I'm still me. Always me.

I repeat my name ad nauseam. Finally, I collapse. The Flesh Flower transformation was terrible, but the peace I felt at the end was wonderful. I want to go back. It's better than this shit, at least.

Being a Flower doesn't require me to think. Doesn't require me to be. I simply exist, and I can stop trying to be alive.

Walking in this desert is a desperate struggle for survival. Repeating my name is a desperate struggle for significance. I just can't take it anymore.

I hear the thudding in the distance. I sit down for the first time in what must've been half a billion years.

I hear the thing getting closer, see its handprints in the sand. I close my eyes and prepare to be torn apart or strangled or crushed, or some other horrible experience.

Hands grab at every part of me. Every joint. Every bone. Holding my eyes open, forcing me to witness this violation of my existence.

I feel my joints snap, hear them pop as they're forced out of socket. The creature stretches me out, each limb going a different direction. It keeps pulling, even after I've stretched as far as I can.

The pain is unspeakable. The Flower was worse, but this… this still isn't easy. I feel my throat tear and it informs me that I've been screaming. I can't hear anymore.

I feel a hand wrap around my throat, as if to shut me up. I try to struggle and thrash but it doesn't work. Another wraps around the necklace and tears it away. I feel the flesh on the back of my neck rip as the chain snaps. The heat against my chest I've grown so accustomed to vanishes.

And then returns. The creature grabs it again and tears it away, only for it disappear from its hand and reappear around my neck. The creature's grip on my body loosens.

It sets me down. My body slowly pulls itself back together, each nerve screaming as my bones slide back into place and my flesh rapidly regrows.

I guess I *can't* die.

The creature doesn't touch me anymore. A hand holds the locket, as if inspecting it, but otherwise the creature keeps its distance.

After a minute of inspection, it gently picks me up and places me on its back. The ridges of its spine dig into me. I'm terrified that I'm about to experience some new kind of horrible painful Hell, but no.

It begins to move, skittering across the dunes as fast as the car. It's moving to the left of the way out. I shout and point, saying that we're moving away from the exit. The creature either ignores me or can't hear me. I don't know if it has ears.

Within an hour we arrive at the way out. The *actual* way out. I scream so hard and so loud I make the creature flinch.

The Third Eternity: Self

The creature picks me up and sets me down on my feet before scampering off. I yell a halfhearted thanks at it as it leaves.

I turn to face the building the creature dropped me off in front of. It's a run down movie theater. The posters out front have all been torn apart. Most of the lights are broken. A flickering red sign reads, "Lakeview Cinema".

I step inside. The smell of mold and rot slams into my nose, making my eyes water. I hold my hospital gown over my face and pick my way across the soggy carpet.

Each step seeps water out of the fabric. I want to vomit. I hope you can't contract diseases in Hell.

Fluorescent lights flicker in the ceiling. I look around at the dilapidated mess of a building. There's only one door, despite the halls stretching off as though there should be more. Ancient popcorn is strewn about the floor, a few of its buckets scattered among it.

Off to my right is a ticket station, to my left a concession stand. Something about their placement feels wrong, as if someone who didn't know what a movie theater looked like tried to design one.

The floorboards creak under the carpet as I walk up to the only door. I give the handle a gentle push and it swings wide open. It's dark inside, a few exit signs casting the only light across rows of empty seats.

I sit down in the exact center, as best as I can. It's always the best seat, and it's not like I'm contending with anyone.

I hear the projector start to hum behind me, sputtering as it whirrs to life. The screen shows a picture of the Moon in a suit standing in the middle of a bunch of lines and shapes. There's text below It, reading, "Please Stand By". The image flickers as a song starts to play.

It's distorted at first, before correcting itself into a cheery tune. The Moon walks into frame, grinning. It laughs, placing a hand on Its stomach as It does so.

Its familiar, sadistic laugh fills the room, making the walls shake and vibrating my seat. When It's done, the image shifts to a blank screen with text on it, like one of those movies from before they had sound.

"This one's going to be easy. All you have to do is find yourself."

The video cuts back to the Moon again. It's leaning forward, wagging a finger at the camera like It's scolding a child. Its laugh fills the room again.

Back to text. "Throughout all of human history in this Cycle, including what you would consider to be the future, there have been 201,364,438,972,331,

704,008 lives."

This time, It's sitting on a chair absentmindedly flipping through a book. It has a monocle on. The childishness of the presentation disgusts me. It feels like It's mocking me, and considering how It's treated me since I got to the desert, I'm sure It is. It laughs again.

"Say a number between 1 and 201,364,438,972,

331,704,008 and you'll relive their life."

It's standing again, staring at a tube TV. It's laugh fills the room once more, even though It's facing away from the camera.

"But I'm not a complete monster. To make it easier on you, I'll split you into a trillion versions of yourself."

It's wagging Its finger again.

"Don't get it twisted, you'll still experience all versions of yourself as if they're the real you. It should make it go faster though."

It's leaning back and cackling, far more animated than the first time. The room rumbles again.

"It'll only be about 200 million a piece. Not so hard, right?"

The Moon is standing closer to the camera, giving a grin and a thumbs up. Its laugh plays once again. Then again. Then again. It's as if an arena of Moons is laughing at me. My chair vibrates so aggressively that my teeth click together hard enough to break most of them.

All at once, the rumbling laughter stops and the video cuts out. I'm left in a deafening silence with a sharp pain in my mouth.

I blink and suddenly find myself looking through a trillion sets of eyes. It's nauseating. Every version of me immediately vomits in the seat in front of us (me?) before sitting back down. I blink, and all of me blink at once.

I try to blink separately, and it feels like trying to do two separate tasks with each hand at the same time… multiplied by a trillion.

It's disgusting.

Me, the prime me, the original me who watched the video with the Moon, takes a deep breath and looks up at the screen. I force every other version of myself to stare at the floor, to try to regain some sense of normalcy.

It's a struggle, like trying to move my eyes separately. It takes a few days to get all trillion of them… of me to listen and look down. Besides the original me, that its. Or what I think is the original me. I can't really tell anymore.

I glance up at the screen, some of my other heads popping up. I force the others back down. It feels so violating to be split like this. Like suddenly having a bug's eye and seeing a thousand versions of the same image. It makes me want to vomit again every time they move.

I say the number one aloud. Immediately, this version of me is slammed into the eyes of a baby being born. Every other version remains staring at the floor, breathing heavily.

I watch myself… no, somebody else… emerge into the light, into a world I haven't seen in so, so very long. The light is blinding, screams escaping my lips. Screams that aren't my own.

It feels like I'm trapped behind the eyes of someone else. I'm a witness, not in control. I watch as things happen, but have no agency.

This baby blinks and looks up into the eyes of its mother. A face that's almost human, but not quite, stares back at me.

This creature looks above my head and makes sounds at the one that birthed me.

Us? Them? I don't know if I should consider this a life I'm living or not. It sure as hell feels like I am. Wherever we are, it's absolutely freezing.

The mother wraps an animal fur around me. It's a little rough, but it's warm. She grunts and hoots at the first face I saw. They talk back and forth for a bit before the first one walks off. The mother coos at us and play with us. The one in control of our body grabs her finger and babbles.

I watch every second of this life. As the child grows up, he's taught to hunt and fight by who I believe is his father. His mother teaches him which fruits are ripe and which aren't, and which plants will poison us.

I watch the first time he looked into a lake and saw his own reflection. He touched his own face, then poked his own nose in the water, watching his face ripple. He understood that it was him.

I watch as he makes his first kill. As he falls in love. As he loses his virginity, as he has kids, as he teaches them to hunt and pick fruit, as he grows sick and old, and as he's eventually killed.

In his final moments, he was hunting with his sons. They were after some kind of large cat that had killed one of his daughters. It got him by the throat. I felt the sharp pain, felt the warm blood oozing down my chest, felt the fear and panic of dying. I heard his sons, *our* sons, scream as they rushed in to kill the beast.

Our vision faded before we got to see if they were safe. Our last thoughts were of protecting our children.

I sit up with and suck air in. I'm hyperventilating, the adrenaline and shock of such a violent death flooding my system with panic. I cough and sputter and try to slow my heart rate. Every version of me does the same. When I've calmed down, I feel… grief. Guilt. Fear. Shame.

I couldn't ensure my children were safe. I failed to protect them, and I don't know what became of them. I may never know, depending on how long it takes to find my own life.

My lip quivers. All of me take a shaky breath at the same time. I look back up the screen, forcing the others to look down again, and say the number two.

This one starts much the same. I turn out to be a kid living in the suburbs with a lovely family, born in 1968. Once again, I watch myself grow. I make friends, fall over and scrape my knee, learn to ride a bike, go on my first date. I didn't even realize I considered this to be me until I turned sixteen.

At some point, I slip off to go to the bathroom. I look at myself in the mirror. I recognize that this is me. Some version of me, at least. I'm living this life. I am the face looking back at me.

That night, I snuck out to meet some friends in the woods. One of them stole a bottle of his dad's scotch and brought it to share. We all got drunk, laughed, and celebrated my birthday. It felt so nice to have friends like this.

We decide to take a little walk through the woods, singing stupid songs and dancing among the trees. None of us are walking straight, but I'm the worst. The birthday boy got to have the most alcohol, after all.

I trip on a rock, stumbling to the ground. It was too dark for me to notice and I was too drunk to pay attention. I had been standing near the edge of a ravine, one filled with rocks and sharp ledges. I slide over the edge before any of my friends have the chance to grab me.

I feel my neck snap on the first impact. I don't feel the rest of the fall. By the time by body has settled at the bottom, my vision is almost completely faded. I die a few moments later.

Once again, I awake in a panic. It takes me a long time to get myself under control. When I finally do, I decide to stop wasting time.

Every single one of me says a different number, starting from three and moving up. When a life is finished, I immediately move onto the next one.

I experience everything humanity has to offer. The highs and the lows. The beautiful and the absolutely atrocious.

I witness the birth of countless children.

I give birth to them, too.

I eat every food.

See every animal.

Ride rollercoasters.

Kiss a boy during prom.

Cheat on my husband.

Cheat on my wife.

Get cheated on more times than I care to count.

Kill someone in self defense.

Go to war.

Kill someone in revenge.

Learn how to sew.

Read books I never knew existed.

Learn languages long since dead.

Kill someone for fun.

Become president and get shot during a motorcade.
Fail to protect the president during a motorcade.
Kill the president during a motorcade.
Witness my own death from a different perspective.
Keep bees.
Run a farm.
Build a car.
Drop bombs on a foreign country.

I know what it's like to do every single thing in human history. I know all there is to know.

The feeling of an atomic blast searing away your flesh.
How to hypnotize chickens.
How to raise children.
What it's like to be beat.
What it's like to see a rainbow for the first time.
What the sun feels like after a long winter.
What an abusive relationship is like.
What it's like to be an abuser.
What it's like to be abused as a child.
The feeling of love.
Losing your virginity in countless ways.
Marrying more people than I could ever remember.
Believing in more gods than I ever knew existed.
The taste of human flesh.
Being tarred and feathered.
Playing the video games I loved as a child a few million times over.
Making those games myself.

How to paint.

How to crochet.

Learning how to kiss from an older girl. I married her and got disowned by my parents for it.

Becoming a priest.

Graduating from every college to ever exist.

Being an alchemist.

And a witch.

And a witch hunter, burning my former self at the stake for daring to be different.

What it's like to be gay.

What it's like to be transmasculine.

What it's like to be transfeminine.

What it's like to be a lesbian.

What it's like to be nonbinary.

What it's like to be agender.

What it's like to be violently homophobic.

What it's like to be violently transphobic.

What it's like to be violently racist.

What it's like to be white, and black, and asian, and hispanic, indigenous to every country, and every other community to ever exist.

What it's like to be the girl I once loved. Turns out, she had a kid with the guy she told me not to worry about.

What it's like to be a child with the eyes of that woman.

What it was like to be my parents.

What it was like to be my brother.

What it was like to deal with me. In every way. I realize that maybe I did deserve this Hell. I was a much worse person than I thought.

What it's like to crucify someone, and what it's like to be crucified.

To be Jesus.

To kill Jesus.

To murder political opposition.

To be murdered for wanting a better world.

To be killed for exposing corruption.

What it's like to be killed for doing nothing at all.

To be murdered to satisfy some sick fuck's desires. That sick fuck being a previous version of me, of course.

To love so many pets that I can't put it into words.

To look at the moon and wonder if life will always hurt this much. If there's ever a way out. If it truly does get better, or if it's suffering until the end. I want to tell myself that there's a light at the end of the tunnel, but me the Observer can't speak to me the Actor.

To die surrounded by loved ones. Something I didn't get to experience in my own life. I think. It's hard to remember how I died. It all feels so blurry, a drop in this ocean of memory. Of this love of life.

To kill myself out of desperation.

To kill myself to avoid punishment for my crimes.

To get away with sins that nobody will ever bring to justice. Except maybe the Moon, considering how my own past eternity has gone.

Witnessing every facet of human existence has filled me with such a love of life that it's impossible to express. It had been so long that I forgot what it was like to live. To really truly live, not this bullshit I found myself in.

The Third Eternity

I have so many regrets. I wish I did so much differently. I'd do anything to be alive again, really truly alive again. To be fair, this wasn't far off.

I watch myself harvest organs.

I kidnap people.

I extort people.

I exploit the poor.

And I cure cancer.

I give back to the community.

I help addicts turn their lives around.

I help bring criminals to justice.

I help bury people's loved ones.

I conquer nations and decay in tombs.

I excavate those tombs in search of history.

I kill a man just for loving someone in a way I don't like.

I get murdered for daring to love.

I write poetry.

And plays.

Books.

Movies.

Create works of art loved for generations.

I travel the world.

I meet the love of my life abroad, and have to spend far too long separated from them. I've felt love unlike any other when I finally got reunited with them.

I've been long lost friends.

I've watched the fall of Rome.

I've been a man, a woman, and everything in between and outside of those metrics.

I've loved everyone in and out of those metrics, too.

Discovered a favorite food.

Or a song that sits with me for years, always reminding me of better days.

Games that make me cry.

Books that make my heart hurt but fill me with an indescribable joy.

I've been the most influential people and the least.

I've suffered every injustice and mental illness.

I been a perpetrator of them, too.

I've been lobotomized more than a few times. It's always a strange feeling to come back to my own body for a few seconds and suddenly regain all my faculties.

I've been blind.

And deaf.

And mute.

And paralyzed.

And a paraplegic.

I've been a loverboy.

A philanderer.

A freak.

Vanilla.

A creator.

A destroyer.

A genius and a fool.

A rocket scientist and a college dropout.

An indie band drummer and a world renowned rockstar.

I've been to more concerts than I can count, and played all of them.

I've seen technology I never could have imagined, played games I never could have predicted.

Seen the world rise and fall over and over.

Seen culture change so, so drastically throughout the ages.

I've been a gardner and a lumberjack.

An environmentalist and an oil tycoon.

Living off of food stamps and buying rockets just for fun.

I've been a monk.

I've been a punk.

I've been an activist and a Pinkerton.

I watched my father die to a wild cat, answering my question about what happened to my sons from my first life.

I've died as a baby too many times to be fair.

I've been a piece of shit.

I've been a saint.

And I've been you. I've seen the world through your eyes, and seen more of your life than you have. No matter how hard it gets, I promise it gets better. I've lived it.

I've bounced around a bit in the numbers. I wanted to make sure It didn't make my life the very last one on the list, and It didn't. Circumstantially, my life was the last one I picked. Or maybe on purpose.

I also discovered that I can't stop watching a life after I started it. I don't mind, though. Sometimes it's nice to go back and relive them. To see old loves. Old friends. Old family. Old pets. People I loved with my whole heart.

It's made me realize just how much I missed in my own life. How many things I took for granted, how many things I refused to explore and experience.

I wasted my life because "I was young, I'll have time to do it later".

And now I'm in Hell, watching what I could've been.

At last, I come to my own life. After watching two hundred one quintillion, three hundred sixty four quadrillion, four hundred thirty eight trillion, nine hundred seventy two billion, three hundred thirty three million, seven hundred four thousand and seven lives, I finally reached my own.

I've seen the good, the bad, and downright fucking disgusting of humanity. And to wrap it all up, I get to watch myself.

I say words I know firsthand hurt their feelings. Do things I know for a fact made them cry. Treat people in ways I know, from experience, makes them feel worthless.

I look into a mirror and see a face that isn't me. Every other life, I've looked into mirrors and seen some part of myself looking back at me. But not this time.

I relive the first diagnosis. The moment I realized my life was going to end far sooner than I ever thought it would. I feel that pit in my stomach, the fear rising in my throat, the heat in my head and chest.

I watch as I deteriorate again. As I fall to pieces and slowly lose the ability to control myself. I feel pathetic. Unspeakably pathetic.

I relive the years I spent in hospitals, constantly poked and prodded by needles. Constantly sent to different rooms for different tests. Watching the debt grow larger and larger the longer I spend in the system.

And then I die alone. Unceremoniously. On a random day, after nothing special happened, having wasted away in a hospital after pushing away everyone who ever tried to love me.

Living as horrible people hurt my heart. Watching myself hate people for being different, watching myself hurt people for the stupidest reasons, watching myself abuse partners and children and elders, all of it was so awful. I hated every second of it.

But living this life again was somehow worse. Not because I was a shittier person. I never ate people or beat children in the life I originally lived, so I'm definitely better off than some of the lives I've experienced through this process.

I think it's because it's my life. While I lived the other lives, I wasn't in control. I knew it wasn't truly me. I was an observer, not the one living. But this life? It was all me. All my choices. I was looking into the mirror and seeing what a mess I made of everything.

And by contrast, experiencing all of the good the world has to offer filled me with so much happiness. I understand life in a way nobody alive ever could. My love for life, for living, for the opportunities and wonders we were capable of made me feel like I was going to burst from joy.

I have become all of humanity, past, present, and future. I have witnessed everything humanity ever will, know everything we ever will. I am humanity itself.

When the reliving ends, I sit alone in the theater. All of me have become one again. I stare at the floor through a single pair of eyes for the first time since all of human history. I don't know who I am anymore.

I want to be all of those people who did wonderful things. Who lived good lives and were good people.

Who took care of those around them and gave back to the community. Who fought for a better world. Who were something more than what circumstance said they were.

And I want to forget about the me that lived. I want nothing to do with that life. I don't know if that's even me anymore.

I'm the amalgamation of everything to ever exist. Every person to ever live, since we were barely human and hunting big cats to avenge our daughters.

I sit there, stewing in my own thoughts. It can't be more than a few minutes, but it feels longer than everything leading up to that very moment combined.

I blink, hard. I keep my eyes closed. When I open them, I'm standing in front of a gaunt, sad looking man. I frown. I never lived as this man, I'm sure of it.

Realization

I try to walk toward the man and slam into some kind of invisible wall. The man is staring at the floor, a blank expression across his face.

He's tall, a little taller than me. He has dark hair and a medium length beard. He's thin, his cheeks sinking into his face and his eyes digging into their sockets. He looks unwell.

And looking closer, he looks… inhuman. His eyes are completely white. Not like he's blind, like he doesn't have irises or pupils.

I feel the necklace pulse around my neck, growing hotter and brighter with each beat. It flies toward the man, snapping itself off of my neck. It goes straight through whatever barrier I ran into before.

I watch as it grows and disfigures. It's glowing as if it's been heated to the point of melting, but morphs itself into the shape of a human… almost.

The glow subsides, leaving behind a humanoid figure. It has four arms and a pair of wings, but otherwise looks like a person. They have fluffy brown hair and wear a toga and sandals. A soft glow surrounds them, as if they're covered in a layer of pure light. They turn to glance back at me, and I realize their face is unseeable.

It's as if I'm looking at nothing. Like an image has been deleted from my vision itself. The face is gone, even though I can see the rest of them clearly. They run toward the gaunt man.

They say something in a language I can't understand. The man looks up for the first time, giving them a warm smile.

The four armed person reaches the man. They gently grab his face with their top hands and pat him down with their bottom hands, the way a person might fret over someone they care about. They say something I can't understand again.

The two of them embrace, a long, tight hug. The four armed creature pulls back and looks the man in the eyes. The man heaves a heavy sigh, holding the four armed person's face with his left hand.

I watch as the man pulls a blade out the belt line of his pants. The four armed creature doesn't seem to notice. I slam against the invisible wall and scream, but they can't hear me.

I watch in horror. All I see is the man's shoulder twitching before the blade is hilt-deep in the four armed person's temple.

They fall to the ground, shaking and twitching. The man stares at what he's done, a sad look on his face. I slam against the barrier again and again. The person's body spasms as the life leaves them. Their light fades.

I stop slamming on the barrier and fall to the floor. I back away from the man, a sob heaving out of my chest. I may not have seen them properly until now, but that person has been with me through everything. Since I escaped the Flower, anyway.

The man's gaze slides over to me. My blood runs cold.

"I'm sorry." His voice startles me. I hear it coming from him, but also in my head. And all around me. It's a strange sensation. I flinch.

He walks toward me. I try to speak but the words are stuck in my throat. I want to scream at him. To curse at him and tell him that he's a monster, to ask him why he killed them. My throat closes up on me and I barely manage a squeak.

"I know you don't understand. That's what this part is for. Please, come sit." The voice feels wrong in my ears. In my mind. I shake my head, my breathing rapid and shallow. The man waves a hand and I'm suddenly sitting in a large leather chair.

The man sits across from me in an identical chair, a table between us. The man is pouring tea into two small cups. I crawl as far back in my chair as I can. I frantically glance around, trying to find the corpse of the person. It seems to be missing.

He slides a cup across the table to me. "I'd ask if you like tea, but I already know that you do. Please, have some. It'll help you calm down. It's your favorite."

My heart thunders in my chest. I slowly reach out and take the cup, retreating back into the safety of my chair with the tea in my hands. My eyes are wide as I stare daggers at the man.

"Why?"

"Why what?"

"Why'd you kill that person?"

The man's eye twitches. "Not how I was hoping to start this conversation, but okay." The man takes a sip of his tea before clearing his throat. He sits up straighter as he speaks. "That is… *was* Juno, an angel. They were my lover several eternities ago." The man sets down his cup. "As for why, it was to protect them. From this." He gestures around the room.

I shake my head. "I don't understand."

"I know." A pause. "I wanted to protect them from God. Either I kill them, or they get trapped in what you just experienced. Forever. And you know firsthand how terrible that can be."

My lip quivers. I don't understand what's happening. I'm terrified and this man is way too calm for having murdered someone. Speaking from personal experience, someone who can murder without care is not a good person.

"Who are you?"

"Lucifer. The Devil. Satan. The Temptor, the Snake in The Garden, the so-called 'King of Hell'." The man sighs. "What you humans understand is only partially true. God cast me down for daring to partake in the act of Creation. For daring to make *you*."

"Wait, what? I thought we were made in God's image. And even if you're telling me the truth, why would God punish you for making humanity?"

He laughs. "God doesn't want free will to exist. That ruins his perfect plan. Free will and God's plan cannot coexist, they're inherently opposites. I dared to make creatures who could think for themselves, and he didn't like that. That's why he cast me down to Hell."

I take a sip of the tea with shaking hands. He was right, it is my favorite tea, and it's the perfect temperature. I swallow. Hard.

"Why did God let us live? Why not just get rid of us after you made us?"

"To make Hell. This place isn't here to punish you, it's here to punish me." He takes a long sip of His tea.

"Because God is a petulant child who was so enraged by my daring to create humanity, he's punishing me. I am forced to sit here and watch my beloved creations suffer. I am forced to feel all of their pain and despair."

He shifts in His seat. "Every soul that comes down here adds to my punishment. To make it worse, God makes a new soul for each human. Souls don't go back to living, they stay here to hurt me forever."

I can feel my heartbeat slowing, the adrenaline and fear wearing off. It's replaced by dread unlike any I've felt before.

"Not even the end of reality can save me," the man continues. "The universe eventually implodes on itself, which sets off the next Big Bang. It's a new eternity's worth of human souls to add to my sentence."

Despite Him being the Devil, I feel bad for Him. I know I probably can't trust what He tells me, but He sounds… sad.

"So why do you have to kill the angel?"

"They tried to save me once, a few realities ago. They tried to break me out of Hell, run away with me. God caught them the moment they stepped into this room. He told me I either kill Juno or they get sent through Hell forever. Now, once every few millenia, I have to murder my lover again."

The more I hear, the more it seems like God is a spiteful, angry person. I frown.

"Why did I get sent to Hell? I know from experience that I am far from the worst person to ever exist."

The man shakes His head. "Heaven isn't real. There is no 'good place' for humanity. God sees all of you as the bastard creation of the Devil, so all of you get to suffer. It doesn't matter who you were in life."

My brow furrows. "Then where is everyone else?"

"Here, same as you. Those doors you passed in the hospital were each someone, stuck in that horrible, disgusting abstraction of the form I made for you. The desert and the forest are full of souls, they're just incredibly large. I doubt you'd find anyone if you spent the rest of time searching through them." He takes another sip.

"How do I get out? And why are you answering all of my questions?"

"Well, the exit appears after I answer all of your questions. It's a part of my punishment. I have to explain to each and every soul why they're being punished. That it's my fault you've experienced this Hell."

I want to cry. I don't really know what else to say. Finally, I settle on, "I see. Is there anything else I should know before I move on?"

"Leave the locket behind next time."

My stomach drops. "Next time?" My thoughts spiral harder than they already were. "How many times have we had this conversation?"

"This is the five thousand and thirty second time for you specifically."

"Then is there really a way out?"

"Yes. Through that door." The man motions to His left, a rectangle of light appearing in the distance. Tears are streaming down his face. "Good luck. I hope you get out safely."

I stand up and thank Him before walking toward the door. I hear sobs escape His lips as I move away from Him.

I stop in front of the light and take a deep breath before stepping through.

The Fourth Eternity: Infinity

I wake with a start, cold sweat drenching my body and my pulse thrumming in my throat. My chest feels tight, barely expanding as I suck in air as hard as I can. I fall off my bed, landing hard on the floor.

I feel like I'm having a panic attack and a stroke at the same time. My whole body seems to be angry, twisting and grinding.

I curl into a ball, slamming a hand against my chest in a feeble attempt to ease the pain. I curl harder, trying to escape the agony.

I feel my bones grind against each other until they crack. I feel my tendons tear and my muscles rip into ribbons. My jaw clenches hard enough to shatter my molars.

I feel every single nerve ending unravel itself. Each and every blood vessel bursting apart, my spine seeming to push its way up toward my skull, curving drastically as it pushes up, up, up and into the bottom of my jaw.

The pain is unbearable. I think I am screaming but think I no longer have lungs to fill with air. My very existence feels like an affront to nature, my body splitting apart into a hellish abomination made of flesh and bone.

My jaw cracks, splitting down the middle. I feel the gap widen as my skull begins to expand, segmenting before unfurling. My very soul wails in agony, but I know it falls on deaf ears. Or no ears at all.

Where are the doctors? Where's my nurse? Where is anybody who could walk into the room and witness what's happening, and at least try to help me?

I wonder which angry, wrathful God I accidentally prayed to that would hear my plea for relief and hand me this instead.

I am crying, though I don't know if it's tears, blood, or some other bodily fluid leaking through my eyes. Eyes that are now facing opposite sides of the room.

I can feel my brain exposed to air. I know it shouldn't physically be possible, but I can *feel* every groove as the AC blows stale air through them.

I pray to gods I never believed in for help. Screaming into the aether for someone to save me… or kill me. I cry out for something to save me from this prison of flesh I have become, to let me out, to free me from this.

Nobody responds. Finally, I realize

I'm in Hell.

My prayers run empty. I'm out of words to say, deities to pray to. How long have I been here now? How long have I been stuck as a monument to suffering? A disgusting amalgamation of every kind of discomfort, every flavor of pain… A criminal violation of my very physical existence.

A physical existence I no longer want to be a part of. My eyes have drooped too far to see the clock. I don't know if it has been days, weeks, even years, or just mere seconds. I yearn for escape.

My brain throbs with every beat of what used to be my heart. The stale air flowing through the grooves of my mind feels violating in a way unknowable to the living.

Living. Am I living? Have I died? It took me until now to realize that I don't consider myself to be alive anymore. Even though thoughts run through my head and I can feel every single nerve in my entire body, I don't think I'm alive.

I try to take a deep breath. I feel my lungs start to expand, but stop. I guess they popped. It doesn't matter, the deep breath helps calm me, at least a little.

I realize struggling is only causing me more pain. Like a dog in a bear trap, the more I tense, the harder I thrash, the more agony shoots through my desecrated body.

My body stopped moving on its own, stopping twisting and grinding. The only thing moving me is me. So,

I let myself sit.

Relax my jaw. Or, whatever's left of it.

Let my tongue sit loose. I feel it fall between the halves of my jaw, hanging down in front of my throat.

Slowly, gently, I let each remaining muscle fiber relax.

I feel the tension fade out of my legs, which seem to have split into hundreds of tendrils that snake across the floor like roots. I don't know what they're searching for, but I really could not care any less.

It takes hours, but finally, I'm able to just sit. To let my body relax. I let myself exist here. Without tensing and thrashing about, the sharp, piercing pain fades into a dull ache. It's uncomfortable and painful, but not unbearable.

I was dying for years before this, I'm used to being in pain and discomfort. Not like this, but still. I just have to get used to this like I got used to that. The hope of adjusting to it is the only thing keeping me sane.

I sit still for days.

My pulse slows. The throbbing in my ears subsides. I can hear again.

A gentle tune fills my mind. I realize my esophagus is whistling, contracting and expanding on its own. It creates a steady hum, a hauntingly beautiful instrument. Since I no longer control my esophagus, I choose to simply listen. I enjoy the music it creates. It gives me something to do besides sit still and think about the pain I'm in.

The tune is familiar, but I can't tell exactly where it's from.

Concrete Corpse

A heavy sigh escapes my lips. I wipe the sweat from my brow with the back of my hand, but it barely helps. I take a seat on what appears to be half of a couch and take a long sip of water out of my canteen.

Working in the Carcinoma fucking sucks. It's not like I'm in any danger, but being in it feels so wrong. It makes my skin crawl and I'm always on edge, as if something could jump out at me at any moment. I take another sip.

Clock Duty is my least favorite kind of Carcinoma work. At least, out of the jobs I've had to do. It's annoying because it's inconsistent, and sometimes you get woken at the strangest hours to get to work on some random floor.

Sometimes the rooms grow with hundreds of clocks covering every surface and we have to chisel them off like a parasite. It's not particularly difficult, it just takes a good bit of effort and an ungodly amount of time.

The worst part of it is the clocks themselves. I'm not sure what exactly they are but they piss me off and make me nervous. Once they're off the wall, they appear to just be a regular clock. Nothing but metal and clockwork. When they're still attached, though, they fight you.

Sometimes they'll tell time wrong. You'll check the time, look away for two minutes, and suddenly it claims its two hours later. Not just one of them. ALL of them. Nobody ever sees the hands move.

The little bastards even infect other time tellers. Watches are banned during Clock Duty because they'll… become one of them? They'll start matching the times of the clocks on the wall. We don't know if that makes them dangerous, so all affected watches get thrown out.

Sometimes the clocks move, too. Some of the little fuckers desperately cling to “life”, running away as fast as they can. I remember the first time I experienced it, I had my crowbar under the lip of a clock and was about to pop it off. I blinked, and in that time, the clock found a way to vanish. Entirely. Out of the room.

I still don’t know where it went.

Clock Duty sucks because it makes you feel crazy. You know they’re just fucking with you, but it feels like you’re losing your grip on reality. Especially when they take your watches. I’m really pissed about the watches.

Someone comes in every hour to let us know how long we’ve been working. It’s the only reliable way to tell the time.

Still, despite all of that, it’s leagues above dealing with the Bloodrooms. My father once took me to watch a workgroup handle a Bloodroom when I was younger, probably in hopes of scaring me straight. It worked.

The smell haunts my nightmares. And the sound.

I stand up and brush off my pants. The Timekeeper walks in and shouts a number. I don’t hear what he says, but it doesn’t really matter to me. I know I still have a long time before my shift is over.

I only have a month left before my work period is done. The day of my birthday, I’m free from this bullshit forever. Until they run out of workers, that is. I’m sure I’ll get sent back someday if we ever have a small generation.

With the declining birth rate and the cancer, I wouldn’t be surprised if I’m forced to work until I’m old. I hear that’s how the old world worked, from before. It sounds like hell.

I pick up my crowbar and get back to it. These clocks aren't going to kill themselves.

I flop onto my bed, the springs screeching in protest at my sudden weight. I sigh into my sheet before curling up into it. It feels so nice to be clean and in bed after a long day in the Carcinoma.

I take a deep breath, the smell of mold and stale linen filling my nostrils. I feel myself start to drift off to sleep, and let myself fall. I'm straddling the line between sleep and wake when the buzzer blares as the steel door grinds open.

"Marcus?"

I grumble as I sit up. "Yeah?"

I don't know why they keep bothering me about him. They feel obligated to update me on his condition, but I genuinely could not care any less about how he's doing.

"He get thrown in the Pit again?"

"The Paragon would like to see you."

I snap to attention. I've never even met him. Why would he want to talk to *me*?

"Uh- yeah, um… what for?" It came out awkward and a lot more hostile than I meant for it to. My pulse is thrumming in my throat. I don't know what I did but I'm afraid of what I'm about to hear.

"He's got a job for you. One of the Divine Mandates." The man motions out toward the hallway. "Please follow me."

Without a word, I do as I'm told. He leads me down several hallways of concrete, all of them with steel mesh flooring. Looking through the mesh only shows unending darkness, even though I know for a fact there's a floor only a few feet below. As we walk, I notice that some of the hallways have more rooms than the last time I walked past. To be fair, I hadn't been down this way in a long time.

We reach a set of stairs and climb up sixteen flights. When I bought my room, they told me it was ten flights below the top. I sigh. It won't be long until my floor becomes a part of the Slums.

Reaching the top of the stairwell, the man holds open a wooden door. It looks out of place in a building like this, some of the only wood in the entire complex. I walk through with a lump in my throat.

The room is smaller than I thought it'd be. A relatively cramped concrete cube, the same metal mesh for a floor. It looks… ordinary. I expected the Paragon to be more vain.

The only furniture in the room is a desk made of steel and an office chair sat behind it. The man in the chair has his face obscured by a mask made of steel. Part of me wonders if the metalworkers made it for him or if he made it himself. The rest of me is terrified.

Two guards stand behind him, each of them armed. How they managed to find guns in this place is beyond me. It terrifies me to imagine what kind of power the Paragon has.

"Um… hi."

The man's head moves slightly, the light reflecting off his mask moving with him. Part of it shines me in the eyes. It feels like an intimidation tactic, and it's working.

"Marcus. I've had my eye on you for some time now. As I understand it, you're a rather capable worker."

I shift my weight, my knees feeling weak. “I uh… I try to be. I do my best to contribute.”

“Yes. That’s a good quality to have.” The man looks down at his desk, sifting through a few papers. He seems to be making a show of not paying any mind to my existence.

“Did you… need me to do something for you,” I swallow. “sir?” The man’s head snaps back to face me as if I just insulted him. I feel my bottom lip quiver slightly under his piercing stare.

He turns around to face his guards, waving a hand dramatically. “Leave us. We have private matters to discuss.” Without a word, the guards nod at the Paragon and march out of the room.

I thought that the men with guns leaving would make me feel better. It had the opposite effect. Being left alone with the Paragon was suffocating.

The Paragon stares at me, examining every feature of my face. His expression hides under his mask. I’ve been holding my breath without realizing it. I feel like my ribcage is going to explode.

The Paragon reaches behind his head and disconnects his mask with a loud *pop*. I watch as the Paragon tosses his mask on the desk and buries his face in his hands.

He has short sandy hair. It feels wrong to see the Paragon like this. Like a person. It’s making me incredibly uncomfortable. I don’t know if seeing his face qualifies as treason or something, but I sure as hell didn’t want to be thrown into the Pit for it.

“Um… are you okay?”

I hear a faint sob escape his lips. My discomfort slowly melts into bewilderment. “Can I… help you?”

He lifts his head and stares into my soul. His blue eyes seem to see right through me, even as tears stream down his cheeks. “Can I be honest with you, Marcus?”

I nod.

“Everything is falling apart. We aren’t able to keep up with the Bloodrooms. We need somewhere to go, but…”

I feel my stomach drop. “But this is the top floor. We don’t have anywhere to go, do we?”

The Paragon- no, the man. He’s not the untouchable Paragon I knew of. The man bites his lip and tenses his jaw. “Not exactly.”

“What?”

“This isn’t the top. Not really. It’s just the top of this stairwell.” The man walks to the back of the room and fumbles around the wall with his hands. He finds a corner, peeling a sheet of… paper? off of the wall. A fire exit door sits on the other side.

“There’s another stairwell. And it leads up. There are probably floors up there, rooms, all of it.”

“That’s perfect then, isn’t it? We can just move everyone up into this new stairwell.”

The man shakes his head, his lips pressed tightly together. His eyes are sunken and dark. He looks tired. “Marcus, do you know what the Bloodroom workers do?”

I nod. “Yeah, my father took me to watch when I was younger.”

"That's not enough anymore. It keeps spreading. More of them keep arriving. Rooms are getting flooded. Entire floors have flooded. And the halls aren't growing anymore."

The man looks around nervously, as if he's being watched. He walks closer to me and leans in, whispering. "Some rooms have been *collapsing*. Do you know what this means?"

I furrow my brow, trying to come up with an answer. It doesn't make any sense. Why would they collapse? "...The building is dying?"

It sounded childish. It sounded stupid, even. It's a building. It's made of concrete and metal. Concrete and metal aren't alive, they can't *die*. The Bloodrooms are just a part of the building, like the void beneath the floor grates-

"Close. The building's already dead." His words interrupt my thoughts, stopping me dead in my tracks. So many thoughts, so many feelings start swirling around in my mind. I don't understand. How? What could have possibly killed it? How does a building die?

The man sees the confusion on my face. "Why do you think we call it the Carcinoma? Where do you think the blood comes from?"

"I don't know! I thought it was just the naming convention. Someone thought it sounded cool, I dunno." I press my palms into my forehead.

There's a long silence. I'm trying to process what I just heard, and the man is just watching me. After a few minutes, I take a deep breath.

"So... what do you want me to do?"

The corner of the man's mouth twitches. His eyes dart around the room. "We've sent expeditions up there before, up the Second Stairwell. None of them have come back. Not a single one." He takes a deep breath, his eyes settling onto mine. "We don't know if they died or if they found a way out. I would like to think they'd send someone back down to get us if they found a way out, though. So I'm pretty sure they all died."

"And you want me to go up there?"

"Pretty much, yeah. I want you to find the way out."

"Have you ever even stepped through that door?"

"Nope. Never not once."

"You know you're asking me to go die, right?"

He pauses, just staring at me for a moment. "If you don't find a way out, we're all going to die regardless."

Well shit. He's not wrong. I pinch the bridge of my nose and exhale loudly through it.

"When do you want me to leave?"

"Right now, preferably."

"What? Why?"

"At the rate the bottom floors are filling with blood, this room will be completely submerged in about a day. Keeping everyone below this room alive and stopping them from rioting will be a full time job. Trust me, you're not the only one who will be having a hard time." He glares at me.

I glare right back. This man is an absolute fraud. I had spent my whole life believing the Paragon to be an infallible pillar of our community. Someone who cannot be questioned, someone chosen by the Divines themselves. But this man was just… pathetic.

I glare at him the whole time I walk toward the door in the back of the room. "I'll do this on one condition."

"A time like this and you really want to bargain? Everyone you know will *die*, Marcus." He sighs, waving a hand dismissively and burying his face in the other. "Fine. What do you want?"

"Take my father out of the Pit. I want him at the highest dry floor until I get back. If I come back and he's not up here with you, I'll let us all drown before I tell you where the exit is."

"Alright, alright. Now hurry, please. We quite literally do not have all day."

I roll my eyes and walk through the door. It looks… like the stairwell I've known my whole life. It's backwards, but it's the same as everything else is. It's properly lit, the concrete seems sturdy… it doesn't feel like I'm about to walk into danger. I hope it stays that way.

I make my way up the stairs, one foot in front of the other. Each footstep echoes in the cramped space. It's three full flights before I find another door.

The door is made of plastic. It's blue, completely solid and opaque. It doesn't cover the top of the doorframe nor the bottom. I've never seen a door like this before.

The stairwell ends here. Off to my left, two steps sit as if the stairway was meant to keep going but the architect changed their mind. The ceiling is only a few feet above them.

I hear static coming from behind the door.

The hair on the back of my neck stands up. This feels wrong. It's the same feeling I get on Clock Duty. Swallowing my fear, I gently press on the door. It swings open with almost no resistance.

I step inside to see… something different. Something new. The concrete I've spent my whole life surrounded by was suddenly replaced by… I don't know what.

Small squares of some strange, shiny material. There's lines between the squares, lines that look similar to concrete. The squares cover every surface, even the ceiling.

There's a band of blue squares in a line in the middle of the walls, wrapping around the entire room. Directly across from me, an empty doorway leads to another room. The air is heavy and damp.

There are no lights in this room, but I can still see. It's almost like the little squares give off the faintest glow. It's dark, but I can make out the shape of the room. There are rectangles, about waist high, that are randomly scattered around the room.

Off to one side, there's a large, dark blue box. I walk up to it and tap it with a finger. It pangs the same way the metal grates do.

There are handles across the box's surface. I glance around the room, unsure of exactly where I am or what I'm doing. With a shaky hand, I reach out and grab the handle closest to me. I gently pull it open, and…

It's empty. A blue metal cage with nothing in it.

I check a few more and they are all completely empty. I don't really understand, but I decide to move on.

I walk to the other end of the room, the source of the static. I find a small stairway down into an area full of water. The static is coming from two holes in the wall that spit water onto the floor, which winds through little trenches scattered throughout the room.

These trenches line a pathway, one that takes a sharp right turn near the end of the room. I begin to take a step forward when I hear something.

Breathing. Heavy breathing. A deep, rattling sound, like the kind I used to make when I was sick as a kid. It's coming from around the corner.

Like it was waiting for me.

As silently as I can, I take a few steps back up to the floor I started on. I should have asked the Paragon to lend me one of his guns for this.

I don't know what's making that noise, but I don't want to find out. Maybe it's just paranoia, but that off feeling hasn't left since I saw the blue door. I feel like I'm in danger.

At the top, I slowly look to my right, as if my muscles tensing might give me away. My gaze slides toward the empty doorframe. I make my way over to it as quietly as I can.

Stepping through the doorway, I walk into… an identical room. But something about it feels off.

I lean back into the previous room to look again. Turning back to this one, I realize that it's mirrored, just like the staircase to get up here.

I slowly walk over to the blue door on the other side, my heartbeat deafeningly loud in my ears. I give it a gentle push. It opens just as easily as before, but gives off a quiet squeak as it swings.

I curse and throw myself through it, toward the lit stairway. For no logical reason, I feel like the light will keep me safe. The stairs continue upward on this end, the two misplaced steps leading down this time.

I hear something from inside the room I came from, like heavy footsteps. They're getting louder. I hold my breath and try to will my heart to beat more gently, every thrum in my ears feeling like a betrayal.

The footsteps stop. Sweat drips down my forehead. I hear them start again, faint and distant. I let go of my breath and take a moment to recover. I lean against the wall in the stairway, tilting my head back.

I couldn't even hear it. I press off the wall to keep moving when I catch a glimpse of blue out of the corner of my eye.

The door. The strange door with gaps in the top and the bottom.

It's opening. Slowly opening more and more. My heart begins to thunder again, adrenaline spiking my entire nervous system.

Without thinking, I throw myself up the stairs. I'm in such a hurry that I'm crawling on all fours, hands slapping steps before my feet follow.

I scramble up the stairs as fast as I can, the cold metal biting into my skin. I hear those heavy footsteps coming behind me, each step sending a deafening *CLANG* up the stairwell.

I keep moving until I can't hear the footsteps anymore. I still haven't found a door, so I guess this is a middle ground between this floor and the last one. I sit down and take a second to breathe.

I didn't see anything, I don't know what it was. Every part of me screamed that it was dangerous, that I should be afraid. I don't understand.

Things here have always been a little strange, what with the clocks and the Bloodrooms and the Pit and whatnot.I'm told buildings in the old world didn't have things like that. Nothing has ever been directly aggressive, though. None of it has been alive.

Or… I guess the Bloodrooms count as being alive, now? I still can't wrap my head around this building being alive. Or. Was alive.

I shake my head. Too many thoughts. I can ponder the intricacies of whatever the hell is happening after I find a way out.

I get up and brush myself off, taking a deep breath. I make my way up the stairs for a few more flights until I reach a familiar fire escape door.

As I slide it open, I hear a terrible screech as a paper covering rips apart. I'm back in the Paragon's office.

With no Paragon.

I sit down in his office chair, realizing that it's kinda awful. I guess the Paragon isn't as capable as I had imagined, even if he got his hands on guns somehow.

I glance around the desk. Papers are haphazardly strewn around, all of them covered in scribbles. I can't tell if this version of the office is different, some alternate version of the Paragon having written these marks, or if his handwriting is abysmal.

Regardless, I can't read what any of them say.

I try the drawer on his desk and I'm pleasantly surprised as it pops right open. I find a gun sitting on the top of a stack of papers.

This is exactly what I needed. A way to protect myself. I don't know what was in that weird room with the water, but I don't want to find out what it wanted to do to me.

I fumble with the gun for a minute, careful to point it away from myself and keep my fingers away from the trigger. I had seen one of the Paragon's guards use a gun before, when I was a lot younger. I saw the blinding flash of light and the horrible sound, and I saw a man fall to the floor. Blood formed a halo around his head. They ended up throwing him into the Pit, if I remember correctly.

Regardless, I knew to be careful with where I aimed it.

I find a button on the side and give it a gentle press, causing part of the gun to slide out to the side. I give this cylinder a gentle tap and it spins. I look through it and see that it's got six holes evenly spaced around the outer edge, and all of them are empty.

I frown. I thought guns needed something in them to work? I push the cylinder back into the gun and stand up, cupping a hand over my left ear and squeezing my right with my shoulder.

I point the gun at the other end of the room and give the trigger a squeeze. It takes more effort than I thought it would, but I manage to pull it. I flinch when it slams into the handle, expecting that deafening roar to ring out through the room.

All I get is a little click. I try again. Another click. I try again and again and again and again. Nothing. My heart sinks. I was really hoping I'd have something to protect myself with.

A thought flashes across my mind. How long have the guards been unable to use their guns? If anyone should have a working one, I'd imagine it would be the Paragon.

Have they been using empty guns to keep us in line? I let out an unamused laugh. How stupid I was to think of the Paragon as anything more than a pathetic man.

I try to slide the gun into my pocket but it doesn't fit. I end up putting it between my thigh and the waistline of my pants. If nothing else, I can throw it.

Turning to the door I hadn't come from, I take a deep breath. I need to keep moving if I hope to find a way out. There's not much else I can really do at this point.

As I make my way up the backwards yet familiar stairwell, I realize that I should be heading toward the residential floors. I might actually be able to sleep.

I had only been on this mission for an hour or two, but it's felt like days. Once the adrenaline from the Water Room faded away, the workday caught up to me and my body tried to drag me down.

Eight flights up and I spot an emergency exit door. If this really is a mirror, then this should be the Elite Housing floor. I crack the door open. The metal screeched as I moved it, making me cringe the whole time. I peek inside.

I hold my breath and listen. I don't know if every part of this mirror has something dangerous in it, or if it was only that floor. I think it might be worse to be unsure than to know I was in constant danger.

I don't hear anything, so I push the door open the rest of the way. It screams yet again. I stop to listen once more.

It might be my mind playing tricks on me. It might be the lack of sleep making me go insane. But I hear it. Faint, raspy breathing from down the hall.

The hallway is well lit but I see nothing. My stomach drops as I realize whatever is making that noise might not be something I can see. I never saw anything in the Water Room, but I didn't take the time to look. My heartbeat fills my ears, drowning out the sound.

I grab the door handle and start to pull it. It slides closer to me, groaning in protest the whole time. I'm watching the gap in the door get smaller and smaller when I hear the footsteps. Fast and heavy. Terrifyingly heavy.

I pull harder. I look up in time to catch a glimpse of whatever is in there as the door slams shut in its face. A fat, pudgy white creature with thick legs and no arms. Wrinkles and rolls of fat make it look shriveled. Its face looked like a person's.

It looked like a person.

I remember what the Paragon said about the past expeditions sent up here. I wonder if they were killed by these things, or if they became them. My whole body trembles, the fear still clouding my mind.

I don't want to die. I don't want to become something like that. I don't know what to do anymore. If the guards really are unable to use their guns, then I don't know how they're going to get up here.

I hear its ragged breathing through the door. I thank the Gods that it doesn't have arms.

I make my way up the stairs, with weak knees and extreme nausea. I just want this to be over. I want to go back to doing

Clock Duty and living peacefully, minding my own business. Why did the Paragon have to pick *me* for this shit?

I sit down in the stairwell, my breath catching in my throat. I pull my knees to my chest, burying my face in them. For the first time since I was a kid, I cry.

It started small. Tiny, pathetic sobs escaping my lips. Tears welling in my eyes, my nose and throat feeling tight. It quickly progresses.

Before long I'm out of control. Tears streaming down my face, snot leaking out of my nose. I make noises I didn't even know I was capable of.

I know it's a terrible idea. I know something's probably going to find me and kill me. I don't care anymore.

Letting myself die hurts less than struggling to live. I don't know how far I have left to go. If entire teams of people couldn't make it, what hope do I have?

I squeeze myself into a tighter ball. I hate it here. I hate the Paragon. I hate everyone who put me in this situation. I hate that I was born in this place. I hate this constant feeling of anxiety.

I feel something tap the top of my head twice. I freeze. It was gentle, like someone trying to get my attention rather than anything wanting to hurt me. I try my hardest not to move.

I feel it again, two little taps on the top of my head. I lift my head, inch by inch, until I'm looking up at… myself.

It's tall, its limbs stretching farther that should be possible. Its torso is the same size as mine, giving it an almost comical look.

Its face looks exactly like mine, save for not having eyelids or a nose. Its eyes bulge out of their sockets, staring directly into my soul.

It seems to inspect me for a moment, tilting its head a little. Its gaze darts around my face, covered in tears and snot, my eyes puffy and red. I'm sure it's hard to tell if I'm its mirror version or not, considering the state I'm in.

"Uh… Hi?"

The creature doesn't react.

"I'm Marcus. Are you… are you also Marcus?"

The creature hesitates before nodding slowly. It lifts a hand and for a moment, I think I'm about to be torn apart. Instead, it just motions for me to follow it.

It's movement is odd, jerky and uncomfortable. Its as if the other me's joints are locked, or fused with its bones.

I stand and follow it up the stairs. It's not like there's anything else for me to do. And I don't want to risk making it angry.

It leads me up the stairs until we reach our floor, the same one I live on in my side. It casually walks through the door and holds it open for me. I step through, looking back at myself and murmuring a thank you. I turn back toward the hall and stop dead in my tracks.

I'm face to face with one of the white things. Its face is a few inches from mine, our noses almost touching. Its eyes and mouth are closed. It stands completely still.

Its eyes and mouth start to open, both widening far beyond human capabilities. There's no eyes, no teeth, no tongue. There's light. Warm yellow light that gets brighter the wider its eyes and mouth grow.

I see something in it. Something in the light. I can't tell what it is, and without realizing it, I'm leaning forward to see it better.

I hear the other me chitter behind me, vocalizing some language I can't even try to understand. In an instant, the white creature's eyes and mouth snap shut.

It huffs, turns around, and walks away. Its heavy footsteps thunder down the hall and out of sight. I barely notice it leave.

My brain feels fuzzy. I feel floaty and lightheaded, but in a good way. I can't seem to think straight, my head feels like its full of cloth.

The other me grabs my shoulder and spins me around, examining me once again. It tilts its head and studies my face. After a few minutes, it seems satisfied.

It directs me down the hall to our room. It ushers me inside and points at the bed before closing the door behind me.

I don't question it. I don't have it in me to question it. I just need to rest. I flop onto the bed, the springs screeching in protest at my sudden weight. I sigh into the sheet before curling up into it.

I take a deep breath, the familiar smell of mold and stale linen filling my nostrils. I laugh. The past few hours have been so unspeakably strange.

I'm laying on my bed, drifting off to sleep again despite being so far from home. How strange it is to see how similar things are on the other side.

Its room even has my same alarm clock. I set it for three hours. I'd love to sleep for a year but I know I don't have all that much time.

My mind wanders to my father. I wonder if he's safe. I wonder if the other version of him is also a belligerent drunk. I wonder if he also took the other me to see the Bloodrooms as a kid. I wonder if they even have the Bloodrooms.

And I wonder where I'm going. In theory, there has to be an end. There has to be a way out, right? I mean, it can't just go on forever. Especially since it stopped growing.

The Paragon said it's dead now, so there's a set limit. There has to be an end that won't move. Will I even be able to find it in time?

Worries cloud my mind as exhaustion catches up with me. Without realizing, I slip away.

I wake with a start, the alarm blaring. I slap it to shut it up and stretch. That was the best nap of my entire life. I yawn and stand up to find myself shin deep in blood. My heart drops.

I was only asleep for a couple hours. How did it flood so fast? Did I ruin it? Are they all dead? I still feel fuzzy, but the crowd of panicked thoughts break through.

I swing the door open and throw myself into the hall, splashing blood all over myself. I look around but I don't see the other me. I don't see anyone. All I see are the walls.

Every wall is covered in cuts, deep gashes in the concrete leaking blood. Every wall looks like a victim of a crime, streaks of blood smeared on every surface. The blood itself is a deep, dark red. Darker than any blood I've seen, even in the Bloodrooms.

Memories slam into my brain like a hammer. Watching as they try to cover the gaps with caulk. Watching them slip and struggle just to fail. A humiliation ritual, a punishment. Every single one of them was barely more than a skeleton, like the very life had been sucked out of them.

One of them looked me in the eyes, reaching out toward me and moaning before falling face first. His face was submerged in the blood. He never got up.

I can't stop myself anymore. I curl over and throw up into the pool of blood. The look in that man's eyes as he looked at me, watching him drown in blood, it was too much. I didn't want to be like him.

I wipe my mouth on my sleeve and push the thoughts down. I work my way down the hall, the blood up to my knees now. It's rising dangerously fast,

I make it to the door, pulling it open only for a torrent of blood to slam into me, knocking me to the ground. My face slips under the surface. Countless whispers, hundreds of voices speaking at once, trying to tell me something… the sound fills my ears and my mind and drowns out every thought.

Familiar voices. Unfamiliar ones. Soft, gentle whispers. Angry, sharp whispers. Loud, quiet, harsh and kind, I can't understand what any of them are saying but I can feel the emotion.

I stand up as fast as I can, pulling the door the rest of the way open. The hall fills with the new supply, the river now waist high. I trudge to the stairs and tear myself away from the pool.

As I step out, parts of it stick to me. Tendons of blood, almost like hands holding me back. They tried to pull me back into the river. I grab the railing and pull as hard as I can, breaking free of their grasp.

I sprint up the stairs, each step wet and sopping. Countless bloody footprints cover the stairs, all of them far larger than anything a human could have made. I hope the other me made it out alright.

The flights seem endless. Ten, twenty, thirty flights go by without a door. At thirty five, I stop to take a break and catch my breath. Not ten minutes pass before I see the pool rising toward me, an angry flood trying to catch its escaped prey. I get back to running up the stairs.

Forty seven flights of stairs have passed, and I'm finally at a door. I throw it open and dart through.

I'm immediately blinded. I think maybe one of those white monsters is trying to show me its light again, but no. I raise a hand and squint, and realize I'm in a massive room. One larger than anything I've seen before.

An entire floor, unbroken by walls. The ceiling extends beyond what I can see. It feels wrong to be in such a wide open room.

And the light… it's coming from a hole in the wall to my left. Bright light shines in and makes my eyes burn. I don't think I've never seen light this color before. It's nothing like the ceiling lights inside.

Actually, it's the same color as light inside the white monster.

I take a few cautious steps into the room, The bloody footprints stopped at the door. Looking closer at the hole in the wall, I see… white bulbous orbs in an endless expanse of blue.

I scan the room, trying to make sense of it all. In the center of the room, a man sits on the ground. He's ancient. A long white beard hangs down from his face, his hair stringy and sparse. It pools on the floor around him.

The man is naked, something stuck in his chest. As I walk closer, I see it's some kind of deformed ball. It has small, fat cylinders sprouting out of it. It's clear, and blood flows through it at a steady pace.

"Hello?" I don't expect a response from someone in such a state, but I figure it's worth a try. Blood's flowing through him, if nothing else. "Are you alright?"

The man lifts his head, his whole body shaking from the effort. He manages a smile. "I've never been better. Come sit with me."

I sit down in front of the man. I know the pool of blood is rising but I can't seem to care right now.

"Who… who are you?" I've never seen this man in my life, but he's clearly like me. Not like… the other me, like some imitation of a person. He's a normal man, just incredibly old.

"I am this building." He says it simply, like it made all the sense in the world.

"What? What do you mean?"

The old man reaches up, tapping the strange orb in his chest with a long, gnarled fingernail. "I'm the Host for this building."

He points up. I look up to see the building's heart, massive and swollen. It's dark, almost black, and it isn't moving. It's wrapped in chains, suspended in the air over this man. Blood slowly drips off its lowest point.

“That used to be mine. I think it belongs to the building now, though.” He laughs but is quickly interrupted by a coughing fit. “Or it *was*. Building couldn’t take it anymore, I suppose.”

My mind is slammed with questions and concerns, something I’ve experienced far too many times since I finished my shift on Clock Duty. I manage to organize them enough to get out a simple question.

“Why?”

The man heaves another cough, his body looking like it might snap under the pressure. “We needed a place to live. Corporations bought all of the housing and make rent impossible to pay. Construction took too long, building more homes wasn’t feasible. Too many people and not enough space for them to live. So they made buildings that grew like people.”

I didn’t understand most of what he said, but I got the impression that this wasn’t something he was in favor of. His nose is scrunched up, countless wrinkles rippling across his face.

“And you’re here to keep it alive?”

“Something like that. Someone was supposed to come disconnect me a long, long time ago. But they never did.” The man’s head hangs low as he speaks, his strength waning. He can’t manage to look at me anymore.

“The building kept growing. I couldn’t stop it without someone else, and it was growing too fast for anyone to come find me." He coughs, blood dribbling down his chin. "At least, I hope that's why they never came for me."

I sit back for a moment, digesting all of this. What a horrible thing to do to someone. I don't understand why they would put this man through this torture just to make places to live. There must've been another option, right?

I sit with the man for a long time. The blue expanse through the hole in the wall turns yellow as I contemplate what to do.

"How do I get out, sir?"

The old man points toward the hole, his arm shaking. "That's the only way out. The only escape."

I stare out of the hole. "What's out there?"

The man laughs. "I forgot you wouldn't know. That yellow, that's called the sky. Those white things are clouds." Another coughing fit. The strange replacement heart in his chest is leaking, blood not filling it all the way anymore.

"You have to jump. You'll be free once you reach the bottom." He pauses, as if unsure of the truth behind his words. "If you stay, you'll drown."

I look back to the man, his breathing ragged and shallow. His whole body shakes. I understand the meaning behind his words, even if he's too afraid to say them.

I lean down and pick the man up. He's so light it makes me wonder if he's real. I carry him like a child over to the hole in the wall, close my eyes, and jump as far as I can.

The air is cold and bites at my skin as it rushes past. The old man laughs in my ear, but I can barely hear it over the gust rushing past me.

"Open your eyes, kid!"

I listen and look up, seeing a giant ball of light in the sky. It peeks out from over the “clouds”, the sky turning beautiful shades of orange and purple. The clouds reflect that light, their texture weaving color like I’ve never seen into the sky.

And for a moment, the world was captivatingly brilliant.

We’re At War, After All

A New Beginning

"Number twelve twenty-two?" The voice is distorted, coming through a filter in the man's mask. The glowing blue goggles scan the room as he marks a note on his clipboard.

I stand up and stride to the end of the room, toward the doorway with the masked man. Countless faces sneer at me as I pass. I can't tell if it's jealousy or anger. Both are justified, to be fair.

I pause in front of the man. "I'm Twelve Twenty-Two." He's a few inches taller than me, and I have to crane my neck to look up into his goggles. I can't see his eyes behind them.

"Follow me." He chirps, the filter in his mask glitching slightly mid-sentence. He turns and walks down the hall, not bothering to hold the door for me. I do as I'm told.

The man's heavy footsteps ring out through the hallway, each echo slamming into my head. The walls are too close for comfort and the sound of his boots is obnoxiously loud.

I imagine its intentional. I'd think the Enforcer getup was designed to strike fear into the general populace as needed, boots and opaque goggles included. The man reaches under his helmet and scratches the back of his neck.

I realize I'm watching him closely. Far too closely. I force myself to tear my gaze away from the man and stare off into space. I'm so used to treating Enforcers like predators, it's hard to break the habit.

The man stops in front of a door, the only door in the entire hall. He opens it and motions for me to go inside. I take a deep breath and step through.

I hear a distorted"Good luck." through his mask. I swallow as hard as I can. My mouth is suddenly very dry. My chest and head feel warm. My heart tries to beat its way out of my chest.

The room is completely dark. I caught a glimpse of a table when I walked in, but the man who led me here took all the light with him when he left.

"Congratulations, Twelve Twenty-Two. You've been selected to become an Enforcer, per the Labor Lottery. Should you choose to accept the job, you will be tested physically and mentally to ensure you are fit for the profession. Do you understand?"

The voice comes from the darkness in front of me. "Yes."

"Do you wish to continue with the onboarding process?"

I hesitate. This isn't a decision I can undo. If I sign on, I'm on for life. Do I really want to be an Enforcer until the day I die?

I lick my lips. "Yes."

"Very good." The lights flash on, completely blinding me. I raise a hand to cover my face and try to blink away the spots, the figure of a short man slowly fading into view.

He's wearing an officer uniform, seemingly a military man. As far as I know, soldiers don't get sent to recruitment duty unless they were severely injured in battle or if they're on the verge of being dishonorably discharged. I wonder which one he is.

"Come with me, Twelve Twenty-Two." The man pushes away from his desk as he speaks, the wheels on his office chair squeaking as he slides away from me. He stands up, even shorter than I thought he was, and walks toward the back of the room. I follow him.

He leads me down a series of dull, white corridors before coming upon a metal exit door. The man opens the door, waiting for me to follow. I freeze a few steps from the threshold.

The man raises an eyebrow underneath his brimmed hat. "Is something wrong, Twelve Twenty-Two?" His face is stern and curled into an intimidating frown, but his voice drips with boredom more than vitriol.

"Ah, uh… nothing's wrong. I just want to make sure, this isn't some elaborate Termination scheme, is it?" I cough into my elbow and stare at the man, trying to hide the fear in my voice.

There's an uncomfortable pause that lasts for far longer than it should've before the man bursts out into laughter. "My friend, we have no need to go through such a process for Termination. Why bother lying and hiding it? No, no. We're getting in a car to go to the Precinct. Now come on, we're going to be late."

The car ride is long and uncomfortable. The man continues to appear as bored as a human possibly could be, while I remained stiff with tension and fear.

I stare out the window at sidewalks, streetlights, and glowing neon signs of the city. My mind runs rampant as I try not to throw up in this man's car.

This new life I was stepping into… it's not one I'm sure I want. Once I step into it, there's no stepping out. It's generally considered a great boon to be selected for Enforcer duty, but now that I'm standing here and staring it in the face,

I'm… terrified. Terrified of becoming what I've always hated.

I catch glimpses of the outside world as we speed past. Plague victims writhing on the floor, giant masses deforming them into an amorphous blob as they're ignored by everyone around them. An Enforcer dragging a woman across the ground, another shooting a man on his knees. A few Deadbeats eating straight out of a dumpster.

Worries fog my mind for the entire ride. I don't want to do this, I know I don't. But should I do it anyway? Reluctantly do the job for my own sake? I'm lost deep in thought when the car slams to a halt.

"We're here. Get out. They'll figure out what to do with you. Good luck, Twelve Twenty-Two." I hope out of the car and turn to ask him where I'm supposed to go.

His tires squeal as he tears away, speeding down the street. He left before I could get a word out. I turn to look up at the entrance to the Precinct.

This is really happening. I'm about to become an Enforcer. It feels absolutely disgusting. I know it's a great thing for me and my family, but I feel like a traitor.

The moment I take a step, an Enforcer comes flying out of the door. He looks around and settles his gaze on me.

"You the new recruit?" His voice crackles through his mask.

"Yes, sir."

The man chuckles. "Let's get you suited up."

I follow him inside as he talks. He leads me through the lobby, past a reception desk and a horde of Enforcers.

“Welcome to the Enforcer Corps. We’re gonna get you fitted for your uniform, get a weapon in your hands, and hopefully get you on your first assignment before the day’s over.”

He leads me through a door in the back of the lobby and through a locker room. I frown at the back of his head. “What about training?”

He cranes his neck to look back at me while we walk. “What training? You don’t need training, you’re an Enforcer.”

“But what about the law? Legal use of force and proper procedure and all of that?”

The man shakes his head. “No need. Your only job is to do what your higher ups say. Don’t think too hard about it.”

The man stops in front of a door. “Here we are. Go talk to Mac, he’ll get you set up.” He pauses for a moment. “Oh, and I’m Eighty-Three. I’m your partner and direct superior. We’ll be seeing a lot of each other.”

I nod and hustle into the room, closing the door behind me. I’m greeted by a small box with a circular stand on the floor and a desk to my right. A man with dark circles under his eyes and an unkept beard sits at the desk with a magazine in his hands.

He doesn’t look up when I enter the room. I wait for a second, expecting him to acknowledge my existence, but he doesn’t.

“Uh… hi.”

His eyes slowly drift up from his magazine. “Hey.”

“Are you Mac?”

“Yep.” He turns back to his magazine.

I shift my weight, standing still suddenly making me very uncomfortable. I don't like Mac very much.

"What uh… what am I supposed to do here?"

Mac points to the circle with his thumb, not bothering to look up. "Get naked. After that, stand in the circle, raise your arms above your head."

I undress quickly and try to cover myself so Mac doesn't see my sensitive areas. He doesn't look up from his magazine.

I walk over to the circle and inspect it. There's two rubber bricks in the middle of the circle, about shoulder width apart. I settle my feet on them and lift my arms.

The machine whirrs to life, eight rods shooting up out of it. The rods spin around me at a blistering pace, a buzz growing louder and louder.

Suddenly, all of the rods start to spit out a filament. As they spin, the rods create a uniform around me. It starts with my legs, slowly inching upward to cover my knees, my hips, my chest, my neck…

"Take a deep breath and hold it, and close your eyes." Mac hasn't bothered to look up. I take a deep breath right as the filament starts making the mask, covering my mouth and nose. I feel it wrap around my head to create the helmet, the fit far tighter than I thought it would be.

The machine winds down, the buzz fading with it. I can barely hear it through the mask. I try to breathe but can't. There's an agonizing pause before the helmet flickers on, the blue light shining through my eyelids. I feel a gentle breeze blowing on my face. I'm finally able to breathe.

"You've got a radio and an AC unit in the helmet, a few layers of hexagonal kevlar mesh lining in the rest of the suit. You're not immortal but you should be okay in most fights."

I glance over at Mac. He's finally looking at me now. His voice has a slight electronic buzz to it through the speaker in my helmet.

"Oh, and you should be a few inches taller with those boots."

"Thanks."

"Anytime."

I leave Mac's room to find Eighty-Three leaning against the wall next to the door. "How's it feel?"

His voice is clear as day, coming through the radio in my helmet.

"Different than I thought it would."

"Yeah, sounds about right." He stands up off the wall and faces me. "We've got an assignment. Normally I'd get you in the range to pick your gun but you'll have to do with the standard issue for now."

I nod, unsure what to say.

"Ah, forgot to tell you. You're number One-Oh-Six now. You gotta learn to respond to that name. Anyway, let's get going."

Eighty-Three waves for me to follow him and walks away.

An Uncomfortable Middle

"Alright One-Oh-Six, this is a simple Illegal call. Should be pretty easy for a first assignment." Eighty-Three jerks the wheel to the side, sending the vehicle careening down an alley.

"What does it entail, exactly?"

"Well, first we're stopping at the Steelworks to take care of Aaron Welch, the adult male of the group. After that, we're heading to the squatting residence to take care of the others."

I don't have it in me to ask what "take care of" meant. I already know, but I'm trying not to think about it. "Alright."

After several more sharp turns down alleyways, roads, and the wrong side of the highway, Eighty-Three slams the brake. The seatbelt tries its hardest to snap my collarbone as my body attempts to throw itself through the windshield. Thankfully, neither were successful.

I climb out of the vehicle and push down the bile rising in my throat. I pull my handgun out of its holster, my hands shaking hard enough to make it rattle.

"Come on, One-Oh-Six. We'll be in and out real quick." Eighty-Three jogs up to the door to the Steelworks, an uncomfortable amount of pep in his step.

I hustle after him. The Steelworks is a thing of beauty, if not horror. Assembly lines for as far as the eye can see, rows upon rows of workers shaping steel into usable materials. Most end up as the outer casings of bombs, though a few end up as household appliances. Very few.

Eighty-Three has his arm around a skinny man's neck. The man adjusts his glasses and says something I can't hear to Eighty-Three. He points across the factory as I walk up to them.

"-ere in row two-eighteen. He goes on break in fifteen if you'd like to wait."

"Nah, we'll go say hi. Come on, One-Oh-Six. Let's get it over with."

He pushes the man away from him and moves with purpose toward the fifth row to my right. I follow him, unsure of what I'm supposed to say or do right now.

Eighty-Three scans each face in the row before coming to a stop in front of a pale, sickly looking man. He's unnaturally thin, his cheeks sunken and his skin a disgusting shade of yellow. He's holding a hammer and trying to force a piece of metal into a U shape.

"Are you Aaron Welch?"

Aaron looks up at Eighty-Three, his gaze distant and uninterested. "Ye-"

Before he's able to finish, a thunderous bang rings out through the room. Time seems to slow to a crawl as I watch Aaron's head split apart.

Before Aaron's body hits the floor, Eighty-Three is already walking toward the door we came in from. His voice is clear as a bell through the radio, but it sounds muffled and distant in my head.

"Come on, One-Oh-Six. I told you we'd make it quick."

I'm hyperventilating and my whole body shakes. I take a few uneasy steps toward the door, my knees weak. I look around for something, anything that can make this situation right.

Someone who can fix this.

Someone who can stop Eighty-Three.

Nobody looked up from their assembly line. Not even the people right next to Aaron, the ones who are currently standing in a pool of his blood.

I want to cry.

I feel panic and dread fill my entire body as we roll to a stop in front of an abandoned house. The windows are boarded and the foundation is crumbling, but the sun already set and a faint light fills the gaps between the boards. They're definitely home.

I try to think of something to say. Something to *do*. I could not care any less if the people in this building are here illegally. It's wrong to murder them like this. It's so wrong.

But if I try to stop Eighty-Three, I'll get arrested. Or I'll be killed for trying to aid an Illegal. Or they'll penalize my family. Or any number of horrible things. Fear feeds into indecision, and my moment to act passes.

They say the only thing good people have to do to let tyrants win is to stay silent and do nothing, and they were right.

Eighty-Three kicks down the door and hurries inside. I rush after him, desperately hoping I can do something. Find one of them and get them out before he finds them, maybe. I don't know. I just know I have to do something, anything.

"We have an adult female, an adolescent male, and two adolescent females. Check upstairs, One-Oh-Six."

I sprint up the stairs with my gun in hand, though I know I have no intention of using it. I hear a scream and a gunshot from downstairs. I flinch.

I hear two more shortly after.

I scour the entire floor top to bottom. There's a children's room, but I don't find a child. I pray to any god that will listen that at least one of the kids is going to be safe.

"Find anything, One-Oh-Six?" His voice is loud over the radio, and loud enough for me to hear his filtered voice shouting up to me from the bottom of the stairs.

"Nothing yet." The words escape my lips as I lean down to look under the bed in the children's room. I lock eyes with a young girl, no older than ten. My blood runs cold.

I hear Eighty-Three's footsteps on the stairs. I don't know what to do. I grab the girl and pull her out from under the bed, putting a finger to where my lips would be on my mask to keep her quiet.

Eighty-Three enters the room, my back to him. I'm standing over a child. Eighty-Three is covered in her mother's blood. I'm uncomfortably aware of my gun in its holster.

"What're you waiting for, One-Oh-Six? Take care of the Illegal and we can be done for the day."

My trembling fingers wrap around the handle of my gun. I pull it out but point it at the floor, my arm hanging loosely by my side.

"Come on, One-Oh-Six. Do your job." His voice is harsher than before, his impatience apparent in his tone.

I don't move. I can't think. My head feels like it's full of static. My chest hurts, like my heart is trying to tear itself apart to punish me for even considering this.

"Either you shoot it right now or the Private Police will get a hold of it." Eighty-Three places a hand on my shoulder, probably an attempt at comforting me. I barely feel it. "You're doing it a kindness by making its death quick."

I know he's right. I know firsthand that he's right. If it's this or SUPP, then there's no doubt that a bullet through the brain is the best thing for her right now. I still can't move.

I've had one experience with the Separatist Union Private Police in my life. When I was young, I was friends with the girl next door, Kaitlyn. We used to play together while our parents were at work. She was my best friend.

One day, the Private Police came knocking while we're playing. They're looking for her. Won't say why. A man in a dark officer's uniform with a kind voice very politely asked her to come with him. He encased her tiny hand in his giant gloved fist, and gently led her out of the house.

A few weeks later, her parents get a cardboard box in the mail. It contains nothing but a handful of her bones. It's all they had to bury her with. I never found out what happened to the rest of her.

When I was older, I was told she got sent to be entertainment at a party for the richest people in the SUA. I never wanted to know what they did for her to end up like that.

I know I need to shoot this little girl. I can't let her go through what Kaitlyn went through. Eighty-Three is yelling in my ear, his normal and filtered voices mixing into a cacophony of rage and pressure.

My heartbeat drowns out every other sound. I can't breathe. I lift the gun slowly, bringing it level with her eyes. She's staring at me over the barrel, tears streaming down her face.

She has her arms wrapped around a little stuffed bear. She's turned her body to protect the bear from me. Her lip quivers but she stares up at me in defiance, refusing to let me hurt her bear.

My heart breaks. She's being so brave. She's caring for something smaller than her at her own expense. Why can't I be like that?

I pull on the trigger as hard as I can, but it barely moves. My whole body is refusing to listen. My heartbeat fades from my ears, Eighty-Three's voice slamming into my head.

I don't hear words. Just screams. Just more noise to add to the static in my brain, the memory of the mother's scream and of Aaron's head disappearing filling my thoughts.

The world grows impossibly loud.

I squeeze harder. The trigger barely moves.

And in a moment, the world becomes perfectly clear. The static vanishes, the pain in my chest fades, and I see with clarity.

I turn as fast as I can, jab the barrel against Eighty-Three's forehead, and try to pull the trigger.

It flies back with no resistance.

An Unfortunate End

I'm staring down at the cuffs clasped around my wrists, panic and fear swirling around in my mind like a storm.

"Well, considering the circumstances, you're facing a pay cut for two weeks. Your next paycheck will be half of what it should be."

I look up for the first time since the interrogation started. "What?"

The man raises his eyebrow. "Is something wrong, One-Oh-Six?"

"A single paycheck at half pay. That's it? I just admitted to killing my boss."

"I mean, it sounds like he deserved it."

"That doesn't change the fact I shot him."

"If you want a longer pay cut period, I can give one to you." He shrugs. "If that'll ease your conscience."

I shake my head. "No, that's not the point. Believe me, I am relieved to not be suffering more serious consequences. I just don't understand."

He leans back in his chair and props his feet on the table. "What's there to understand? You're getting a punishment for your misbehavior at work."

"Yes, but I killed a coworker for doing his job. I protected what you all deem to be a criminal at the expense of his life. Why do you not seem to care?"

The man takes a long drag off of his cigarette. "Well, the little girl you were trying to protect is in SUPP custody now.

It's a shame we couldn't get the other children in the house to them, but you made sure he paid for that already."

I grit my teeth hard enough to make one of them crack. I sure as hell didn't shoot him for not letting SUPP get their hands on them. I pray the girl dies quickly and painlessly. I know there's nobody listening.

"Besides, who cares if an Enforcer dies on the job? There's always some bottom feeder scrambling for the position, it won't be hard to replace him."

The man waves a hand and my handcuffs beep loudly. They hiss before snapping apart and falling onto the table with a heavy thud.

"Don't worry too much about it. The family's not going to try to get revenge on you and you're not going to be shunned in the workplace or anything. Nobody cares that he's gone just like nobody cares about a missing Illegal family. People have bigger issues to worry about than some dead asshole."

He shoots me a playful grin that makes my skin crawl. I've never felt so violated by a friendly gesture. "We're at war, after all."

Acknowledgements

Thank you to everyone who supported me while I created this collection of stories. I appreciate each and every one of you for your contributions and for putting up with me throughout its creation.

A special thank you to my family for always taking care of me and for giving me the environment to be able to make stories. I know not everyone is lucky enough to have parents that support creatives.

And a massive thank you to both my brother and my friend Elliot Haschke for helping me refine my ideas. Without them, the Second and Third Eternities, as well as the meeting with Lucifer, would not be what they are today.

When I started writing these stories, I never expected it to actually get finished. I have a bad habit of starting too many projects and struggling to actually get any of them done.

Satan Weeps is partially my take on the concept behind Dante's *Inferno*, and partially a remnant of my feelings regarding faith.

I am a former Christian, and I never really agreed with many of the concepts behind it. Things like the conflict between free will and God's plan, the existence of evil, and the concept of an eternal punishment for a finite crime were things I struggled to align myself with.

I think part of the reason I made this story was to finally let go of it all. Put my thoughts into words, even if through a story, and finally completely step away from it.

This is not an attempt to disparage the faith, by any means. It's an interpretation of the concepts presented and a twist on a classic story. I have been hurt on behalf of Christianity before, and know many who have had similar experiences, but I am not attempting to start a fight.

Concrete Corpse is based on a dream I had while in the process of writing Satan Weeps. It's as close of a recreation as I was able to make of the events of that dream.

To this day, I'm still unsure of what exactly the meaning behind the dream was. I took some creative liberties to write the story, assigning meaning to the parts that didn't have one clearly provided. Still, I think about that dream all the time.

We're At War, After All is, unfortunately, based on the current state of the world. I take care to be an informed citizen, and much to my dismay, being an informed citizen feels like a cruel and unusual form of punishment. Every headline is like a hot iron to my brain.

I've watched the only home I've known devolve further and further into a bigger mess than it already was, and I've felt powerless to stop it. I guess this story is a strange attempt to say something about it. To voice those feelings.

We're At War, After All was partially inspired by the wonderfully disturbing phenomenon of reading old dystopia. The kinds of dystopian fiction we used to write decades ago talks about the kinds of things we're doing right now. What was once an unfathomably evil future is a current reality.

It's also loosely inspired by Papers, Please and Aneurism 4.

Lastly, I would like to thank all of you for taking the time to read Dystopian Heart, and especially for reading the Acknowledgements. I hope you all are doing well, and remember, "No matter how hard it gets, I promise it gets better."

www.ingramcontent.com/pod-product-compliance
Lightning Source LLC
LaVergne TN
LVHW090615110826
845146LV00001B/397

9798995261308